The Bobbsey Twins
at the Seashore

The Bobbsey Twins at the Seashore

by Laura Lee Hope

Wilder Publications, LLC.
PO Box 3005
Radford VA 24143-3005

ISBN 10: 1-61720-307-6
ISBN 13: 978-1-61720-307-7

Table of Contents:

Chasing the Duck

"Suah's yo' lib, we do keep a-movin'!" cried Dinah, as she climbed into the big depot wagon.

"We didn't forget Snoop this time," exclaimed Freddie, following close on Dinah's heels, with the box containing Snoop, his pet cat, who always went traveling with the little fellow.

"I'm glad I covered up the ferns with wet paper," Flossie remarked, "for this sun would surely kill them if it could get at them."

"Bert, you may carry my satchel," said Mrs. Bobbsey, "and be careful, as there are some glasses of jelly in it, you know."

"I wish I had put my hat in my trunk," remarked Nan. "I'm sure someone will sit on this box and smash it before we get there."

"Now, all ready!" called Uncle Daniel, as he prepared to start old Bill, the horse.

"Wait a minute!" Aunt Sarah ordered. "There was another box, I'm sure. Freddie, didn't you fix that blue shoe box to bring along?"

"Oh, yes, that's my little duck, Downy. Get him quick, somebody, he's on the sofa in the bay window!"

Bert climbed out and lost no time in securing the missing box.

"Now we are all ready this time," Mr. Bobbsey declared, while Bill started on his usual trot down the country road to the depot.

The Bobbseys were leaving the country for the seashore. As told in our first volume, "The Bobbsey Twins," the little family consisted of two pairs of twins, Nan and Bert, age eight, dark and handsome, and as like as two peas, and Flossie and Freddie, age four, as light as the others were dark, and "just exactly chums," as Flossie always declared.

The Bobbsey twins lived at Lakeport, where Mr. Richard Bobbsey had large lumber yards. The mother and father were quite young themselves, and so enjoyed the good times that came as naturally as sunshine to the little Bobbseys. Dinah, the colored maid, had been with the family so long the children at Lakeport called her Dinah Bobbsey, although her real name was Mrs. Sam Johnston, and her husband, Sam, was the man of all work about the Bobbsey home.

Our first volume told all about the Lakeport home, and our second book, "The Bobbsey Twins in the Country," was the story of the Bobbseys on a visit to Aunt Sarah and Uncle Daniel Bobbsey in their beautiful country home at

Meadow Brook. Here Cousin Harry, a boy Bert's age, shared all the sports with the family from Lakeport. Now the Lakeport Bobbseys were leaving Meadow Brook, to spend the month of August with Uncle William and Aunt Emily Minturn at their seashore home, called Ocean Cliff, located near the village of Sunset Beach. There they were also to meet their cousin, Dorothy Minturn, who was just a year older than Nan.

It was a beautiful morning, the very first day of August, that our little party started off. Along the Meadow Brook road everybody called out "Good-by!" for in the small country place all the Bobbseys were well known, and even those from Lakeport had many friends there.

Nettie Prentice, the one poor child in the immediate neighborhood (she only lived two farms away from Aunt Sarah), ran out to the wagon as Uncle Daniel hurried old Bill to the depot.

"Oh, here, Nan!" she called. "Do take these flowers if you can carry them. They are in wet cotton battin at the stems, and they won't fade a bit all day," and Nettie offered to Nan a gorgeous bouquet of lovely pure white, waxy lilies, that grow so many on a stalk and have such a delicious fragrance. Nettie's house was an old homestead, and there delicate blooms crowded around the sitting-room window.

Nan let her hatbox down and took the flowers.

"These are lovely, Nettie," she exclaimed; "I'll take them, no matter how I carry them. Thank you so much, and I hope I'll see you next summer."

"Yes, do come out again!" Nettie faltered, for she would miss Nan, the city girl had always been so kind—even lent her one of her own dresses for the wonderful Fourth of July parade.

"Maybe you will come down to the beach on an excursion," called Nan, as Bill started off again with no time to lose.

"I don't think so," answered Nettie, for she had never been on an excursion—poor people can rarely afford to spend money for such pleasures.

"I've got my duck," called Freddie to the little girl, who had given the little creature to Freddie at the farewell party as a souvenir of Meadow Brook.

"Have you?" laughed Nettie. "Give him plenty of water, Freddie, let him loose in the ocean for a swim!" Then Nettie ran back to her home duties.

"Queer," remarked Nan, as they hurried on. "The two girls I thought the most of in Meadow Brook were poor: Nettie Prentice, and Nellie the little cash girl at the fresh-air camp. Somehow, poor girls seem so real and they talk to you so close—I mean they seem to just speak right out of their eyes and hearts."

"That's what we call sincerity, daughter," said Mrs. Bobbsey. "You see, children who have trials learn to appreciate more keenly than we, who have everything we need. That appreciation shows in their eyes, and so they seem closer to you, as you say."

"Oh! oh! oh!" screamed Freddie, "I think my duck is choked. He's got his head out the hole. Take Snoop, quick, Bert, till I get Downy in again," and the poor little fellow looked as scared as did the duck with his "head out of the hole."

"He can't get it in again," cried Freddie, pushing gently on the little lump of down with the queer yellow bill—the duck's head. "The hole ain't big enough and he'll surely choke in it."

"Tear the cardboard down," said Bert. "That's easy enough," and the older brother, coming to the rescue, put his fingers under the choking neck, gave the paper box a jerk, and freed poor Downy.

"When we get to the depot we will have to paste some paper over the tear," continued Bert, "or Downy will get out further next time."

"Here we are," called Uncle Daniel, pulling up to the old station.

"I'll attend to the baggage," announced Mr. Bobbsey, "while you folks all go to the farther end of the platform. Our car will stop there."

For a little place like Meadow Brook seven people getting on the Express seemed like an excursion, and Dave, the lame old agent, hobbled about with some consequence, as he gave the man in the baggage car instruction about the trunk and valises. During that brief period, Harry, Aunt Sarah, and Uncle Daniel were all busy with "good-byes": Aunt Sarah giving Flossie one kiss more, and Uncle Daniel tossing Freddie up in the air in spite of the danger to Downy, the duck.

"All aboard!" called the conductor.

"Good-by!"

"Good-by!"

"Come and see us at Christmas!" called Bert to Harry.

"I may go down to the beach!" answered Harry while the train brakes flew off.

"We will expect you Thanksgiving," Mrs. Bobbsey nodded out the window to Aunt Sarah.

"I'll come if I can," called back the other.

"Good-by! Good-by!"

"Now, let us all watch out for the last look at dear old Meadow Brook," exclaimed Nan, standing up by the window.

"Let Snoop see!" said Freddie, with his hand on the cover of the kitten's box.

"Oh, no!" called everybody at once. "If you let that cat out we will have just as much trouble as we did coming up. Keep him in his box."

"He would like to see too," pouted Freddie. "Snoop liked Meadow Brook. Didn't you, Snoopy!" putting his nose close to the holes in the box.

"I suppose by the time we come back from the beach Freddie will have a regular menagerie," said Bert, with a laugh. "He had a kitten first, now he has a kitten and a duck, and next he'll have a kitten, a duck, and a—"

"Sea-serpent," put in Freddie, believing that he might get such a monster if he cared to possess one.

"There goes the last of Meadow Brook," sighed Nan, as the train rounded a curve and slowed up on a pretty bridge. "And we did have such a lovely time there!"

"Isn't it going to be just as nice at the ocean?" Freddie inquired, with some concern.

"We hope so," his mother replied, "but sister Nan always likes to be grateful for what she has enjoyed."

"So am I," insisted the little fellow, not really knowing what he meant himself.

"I likes dis yere car de best," spoke up Dinah, looking around at the ordinary day coach, the kind used in short journeys. "De red velvet seats seems de most homey," she went on, throwing her kinky head back, "and I likes to lean back wit'out tumbling ober."

"And there's more to see," agreed Bert. "In the Pullman cars there are so few people and they're always—"

"Proud," put in Flossie.

"Yes, they seem so," declared her brother, "but see all the people in this car, just eating and sleeping and enjoying themselves."

Now in our last book, "The Bobbsey Twins in the Country," we told about the trip to Meadow Brook in the Pullman car, and how Snoop, the kitten, got out of his box, and had some queer experiences. This time our friends were traveling in the car with the ordinary passengers, and, of course, as Bert said, there was more to be seen and the sights were different.

"It is splendid to have so much room," declared Mrs. Bobbsey, for Nan and Flossie had a big seat turned towards Bert and Freddie's, while Dinah had a seat all to herself (with some boxes of course), and Mr. and Mrs. Bobbsey had another seat. The high-back, broad plush seats gave more room than the narrow, revolving chairs, besides, the day coach afforded so much more freedom for children.

"What a cute little baby!" exclaimed Nan, referring to a tiny tot sleeping under a big white netting, across the aisle.

"We must be quiet," said Mrs. Bobbsey, "and let the little baby sleep. It is hard to travel in hot weather."

"Don't you think the duck should have a drink?" suggested Mr. Bobbsey. "You have a little cup for him, haven't you, Freddie?"

"Yep!" answered Freddie, promptly, pulling the cover off Downy's box.

Instantly the duck flew out!

"Oh ! oh! oh!" yelled everybody, as the little white bird went flying out through the car. First he rested on the seat, then he tried to get through the window. Somebody near by thought he had him, but the duck dodged, and made straight for the looking glass at the end of the car.

"Oh, do get him, somebody!" cried Freddie, while the other strange children in the car yelled in delight at the fun.

"He's kissing himself in the looking glass," declared one youngster, as the frightened little duck flapped his wings helplessly against the mirror.

"He thinks it's another duck," called a boy from the back of the car, clapping his hands in glee.

Mr. Bobbsey had gone up carefully with his soft hat in his hand. Everybody stopped talking, so the duck would keep in its place.

Nan held Freddie and insisted on him not speaking a word.

Mr. Bobbsey went as cautiously as possible. One step more and he would have had the duck.

He raised his hand with the open hat—and brought it down on the looking glass!

The duck was now gazing down from the chandelier!

"Ha! ha! ha!" the boys laughed, "that's a wild duck, sure!"

"Who's got a gun!" the boy in the back hollered.

"Oh, will they shoot my duck!" cried Freddie, in real tears.

"No, they're only making fun," said Bert. "You keep quiet and we will get him all right."

By this time almost everyone in the car had joined in the duck hunt, while the frightened little bird seemed about ready to surrender. Downy had chosen the highest hanging lamps as his point of vantage, and from there he attempted to ward off all attacks of the enemy. No matter what was thrown at him he simply flew around the lamp.

As it was a warm day, chasing the duck was rather too vigorous exercise to be enjoyable within the close confines of a poorly ventilated car, but that bird had to be caught somehow.

"Oh, the net!" cried Bert, "that mosquito netting over there. We could stretch it up and surely catch him."

This was a happy thought. The baby, of course, was awake and joined in the excitement, so that her big white mosquito netting was readily placed at the disposal of the duck hunters.

A boy named Will offered to help Bert.

"I'll hold one end here," said Will, "and you can stretch yours opposite, so we will screen off half of the car, then when he comes this way we can readily bag him."

Will was somewhat older than Bert, and had been used to hunting, so that the present emergency was sport to him.

The boys now brought the netting straight across the car like a big white screen, for each held his hands up high, besides standing on the arm of the car seats.

"Now drive him this way," called Bert to his father and the men who were helping him.

"Shoo! Shoo! Shoo!" yelled everybody, throwing hats, books, and newspapers at the poor lost duck.

"Shoo!" again called a little old lady, actually letting her black silk bag fly at the lamp.

Of course poor Downy had to shoo, right into the net!

Bert and Will brought up the four ends of the trap and Downy flopped.

"That's the time we bagged our game," laughed Will, while everybody shouted and clapped, for it does not take much to afford real amusement to passengers, who are traveling and can see little but the other people, the conductor, and newspapers.

"We've got him at last," cried Freddie in real glee, for he loved the little duck and feared losing his companionship.

"And he will have to have his meals served in his room for the rest of his trip," laughed Mrs. Bobbsey, as the tired little Downy was once more put in his perforated box, along the side of the tin dipper of water, which surely the poor duck needed by this time.

A Traveling Menagerie

It took some time for the people to get settled down again, for all had enjoyed the fun with the duck. The boys wanted Freddie to let him out of the box, on the quiet, but Bert overheard the plot and put a stop to it. Then, when the strange youngsters got better acquainted, and learned that the other box contained a little black kitten, they insisted on seeing it.

"We'll hold him tight," declared the boy from the back seat, "and nothing will happen to him."

" But you don't know Snoop," insisted Bert. "We nearly lost him coming up in the train, and he's the biggest member of Freddie's menagerie, so we have to take good care of him."

Mr. Bobbsey, too, insisted that the cat should not be taken out of the box; so the boys reluctantly gave in.

"Now let us look around a little," suggested Mrs. Bobbsey, when quiet had come again, and only the rolling of the train and an occasional shrill whistle broke in on the continuous rumble of the day's journey.

"Yes, Dinah can watch the things and we can look through the other cars," agreed Mr. Bobbsey. "We might find someone we know going down to the shore."

"Be awful careful of Snoop and Downy," cautioned Freddie, as Dinah took up her picket duty. "Look out the boys don't get 'em," with a wise look at the youngsters, who were spoiling for more sport of some kind.

"Dis yeah circus won't move 'way from Dinah," she laughed. "When I goes on de police fo'ce I takes good care ob my beat, and you needn't be a-worryin-', Freddie, de Snoopy kitty cat and de Downy duck will be heah when you comes back," and she nodded her wooly head in real earnest.

It was an easy matter to go from one car to the other as they were vestibuled, so that the Bobbsey family made a tour of the entire train, the boys with their father even going through the smoker into the baggage car, and having a chance to see what their own trunk looked like with a couple of railroad men sitting on it.

"Don't you want a job?" the baggagemaster asked Freddie. "We need a man about your size to lift trunks off the cars for us."

Of course the man was only joking, but Freddie always felt like a real man and he answered promptly:

"Nope, I'm goin' to be a fireman. I've put lots of fires out already, besides gettin' awful hurted on the ropes with 'Frisky.'"

"Frisky, who is he?" inquired the men.

"Why, our cow out in Meadow Brook. Don't you know Frisky?" and Freddie looked very much surprised that two grown-up people had never met the cow that had given him so much trouble.

"Why didn't you bring him along?" the men asked further.

"Have you got a cow car?" Freddie asked in turn.

"Yes, we have. Would you like to see one?" went on one of the railroaders. "If your papa will bring you out on the platform at the next stop, I'll show you how our cows travel."

Mr. Bobbsey promised to do this, and the party moved back to meet Nan, Flossie, and their mamma. Freddie told them at once about his promised excursion to the cattle car, and, of course, the others wanted to see, too.

"If we stop for a few minutes you may all come out," Mr. Bobbsey said. "But it is always risky to get off and have to scramble to get back again. Sometimes they promise us five minutes and give us two, taking the other three to make up for lost time."

The train gave a jerk, and the next minute they drew up to a little way station.

"Here we are, come now," called Mr. Bobbsey, picking Freddie up in his arms, and telling the others to hurry after him.

"Oh, there go the boys from our car!" called Bert, as quite a party of youngsters alighted. "They must be going on a picnic; see their lunch boxes."

"I hope Snoop is all right," Freddie reflected, seeing all the lunch boxes that looked so much like Snoop's cage.

"Come on, little fellow," called the baggage man, "we only have a few minutes."

Then they took Freddie to the rear car and showed him a big cage of cows—it was a cage made of slates, with openings between, and through the openings could be seen the crowded cattle.

"Oh, I would never put Frisky in a place like that," declared Freddie; "he wouldn't have room to move."

"There is not much room, that's a fact," agreed the man. "But you see cows are not first-class passengers."

"But they are good, and know how to play, and they give milk," said Freddie, speaking up bravely for his country friends. "What are you going to do with all of these cows'"

"I don't know," replied the man, not just wanting to talk about beefsteak. "Maybe they're going out to the pasture."

One pretty little cow tried to put her head out through the bars, and Bert managed to give her a couple of crackers from his pocket. She nibbled them up and bobbed her head as if to say:

"Thank you, I was very hungry."

"They are awfully crowded," Nan ventured, "and it must be dreadful to be packed in so. How do they manage to get a drink?"

"They will be watered to-night," replied the man, and then the Bobbseys had to all hurry to get on the train again, for the locomotive whistle had blown and the bell was ringing.

They found Dinah with her face pressed close to the window pane, enjoying the sights on the platform.

"I specked you was clean gone and left me," she laughed. "S'pose you saw lots of circuses, Freddie?"

"A whole carful," he answered, "but, Dinah," he went on, looking scared, "where's Snoop?"

The box was gone!

"Right where you left him," she declared. "I nebber left dis yeah spot, and nobody doan come ter steal de Snoopy kitty cat."

Dinah was crawling around much excited, looking for the missing box. Bert, Nan, and Flossie, of course, all rummaged about, and even Mr. and Mrs. Bobbsey joined in the search. But there was no box to be found.

"Oh, the boys have stoled my cat!" wailed Freddie. "I dust knowed they would!" and he cried outright, for Snoop was a dear companion of the little fellow, and why should he not cry at losing his pet?

"Now wait," commanded his father, "we must not give up so easily. Perhaps the boys hid him some place."

"But suah's you lib I nebber did leab dis yeah seat," insisted Dinah, which was very true. But how could she watch those boys and keep her face so close to the window? Besides, a train makes lots of noise to hide boys' pranks.

"Now, we will begin a systematic search," said Mr. Bobbsey, who had already found out from the conductor and brakeman that they knew nothing about the lost box. "We will look in and under every seat. Then we will go through all the baggage in the hangers" (meaning the overhead wire baskets), "and see if we cannot find Snoop."

The other passengers were very kind and all helped in the hunt. The old lady who had thrown her hand bag at Downy thought she had seen a boy come in the door at the far end of the car, and go out again quickly, but otherwise no one could give any information that would lead to the discovery of the person or parties who had stolen Snoop.

All kinds of traveling necessities were upset in the search. Some jelly got spilled, some fresh country eggs were cracked, but everybody was good-natured and no one complained.

Yet, after a thorough overhauling of the entire car there was no Snoop to be found!

"He's gone!" they all admitted, the children falling into tears, while the older people looked troubled.

"They could hardly have stolen him," Mr. Bobbsey reflected, "and the conductor is sure not one of those boys went in another car, for they all left the train at Ramsley's."

"I don't care!" cried Freddie, aloud, "I'll just have every one of them arrested when we get to Auntie's. I knowed they had Snoop in their boxes."

How Snoop could be "in boxes" and how the boys could be found at Auntie's were two much mixed points, but no one bothered Freddie about such trifles in his present grief.

"Why doan you call dat kitty cat?" suggested Dinah, for all this time no one had thought of that.

"I couldn't," answered Freddie, "'cause he ain't here to call." And he went on crying.

"Snoop! Snoop! Snoop Cat!" called Dinah, but there was no familiar "me-ow" to answer her.

"Now, Freddie boy," she insisted, "if dat cat is alibe he will answer if youse call him, so just you stop a-sniffing and come along. Dere's a good chile," and she patted him in her old way. "Come wit Dinah and we will find Snoop."

With a faint heart the little fellow started to call, beginning at the front door and walking slowly along toward the rear.

"Stoop down now and den," ordered Dinah, "cause he might be hiding, you know."

Freddie had reached the rear door and he stopped.

"Now jist gib one more good call" said Dinah, and Freddie did.

"Snoop! Snoop!" he called.

"Me-ow," came a faint answer.

"Oh, I heard him!" cried Freddie.

"So did I!" declared Dinah.

Instantly all the other Bobbseys were on the scene.

"He's somewhere down here," said Dinah. "Call him, Freddie!"

"Snoop! Snoop!" called the boy again.

"Me-ow—me-ow!" came a distant answer.

"In the stove!" declared Bert, jerking open the door of the stove, which, of course, was not used in summer, and bringing out the poor, frightened, little cat.

Railroad Tennis

"Oh, poor little Snoop!" whispered Freddie, right into his kitten's ear. "I'm so glad I got you back again!"

"So are we all," said a kind lady passenger who had been in the searching party. "You have had quite some trouble for a small boy, with two animals to take care of."

Everybody seemed pleased that the mischievous boys' pranks had not hurt the cat, for Snoop was safe enough in the stove, only, of course, it was very dark and close in there, and Snoop thought he surely was deserted by all his good friends. Perhaps he expected Freddie would find him, at any rate he immediately started in to "purr-rr," in a cat's way of talking, when Freddie took him in his arms, and fondled him.

"We had better have our lunch now," suggested Mrs. Bobbsey, "I'm sure the children are hungry."

"It's just like a picnic," remarked Flossie, when Dinah handed around the paper napkins and Mrs. Bobbsey served out the chicken and cold-tongue sandwiches. There were olives and celery too, besides apples and early peaches from Uncle Daniel's farm.

"Let us look at the timetable, see where we are now, and then see where we will be when we finish," proposed Bert.

"Oh yes," said Nan, "let us see how many miles it takes to eat a sandwich."

Mr. Bobbsey offered one to the conductor, who just came to punch tickets.

"This is not the regular business man's five-minute lunch, but the five-mile article seems more enjoyable," said Mr. Bobbsey.

"Easier digested," agreed the conductor, accepting a sandwich. "You had good chickens out at Meadow Brook," he went on, complimenting the tasty morsel he was chewing with so much relish.

"Yes, and ducks," said Freddie, which remark made everybody laugh, for it brought to mind the funny adventure of little white Downy, the duck.

"They certainly can fly," said the conductor with a smile, as he went along with a polite bow to the sandwich party.

Bert had attended to the wants of the animals, not trusting Freddie to open the boxes. Snoop got a chicken leg and Downy had some of his own soft food, that had been prepared by Aunt Sarah and carried along in a small tin can.

"Well, I'se done," announced Dinah, picking up her crumbs in her napkins. "Bert, how many miles you say it takes me to eat?"

"Let me see! Five, eight, twelve, fourteen: well, I guess Dinah, you had fifteen miles of a chicken sandwich."

"An' you go 'long!" she protested. "'Taint no sech thing. I ain't got sich a long appetite as date. Fifteen miles! Lan'a massa! whot you take me fo?"

Everybody laughed and the children clapped hands at the length of Dinah's appetite, but when the others had finished they found their own were even longer than the maid's, the average being eighteen miles!

"When will we get to Aunt Emily's?" Flossie asked, growing tired over the day's journey.

"Not until night," her father answered. "When we leave the train we will have quite a way to go by stage. We could go all the way by train, but it would be a long distance around, and I think the stage ride in the fresh air will do us good."

"Oh yes, let's go by the stage," pleaded Freddie, to whom the word stage was a stranger, except in the way it had been used at the Meadow Brook circus.

"This stage will be a great, big wagon," Bert told him, "with seats along the sides."

"Can I sit up top and drive?" the little one asked.

"Maybe the man will let you sit by him," answered Mr. Bobbsey, "but you could hardly drive a big horse over those rough roads."

The train came to a standstill, just then, on a switch. There was no station, but the shore train had taken on another section.

"Can Flossie and I walk through that new car?" Nan asked, as the cars had been separated and the new section joined to that directly back of the one which the Bobbseys were in.

"Why, yes, if you are very careful," the mother replied, and so the two little girls started off.

Dinah took Freddie on her lap and told him his favorite story about "Pickin' cotton in de Souf," and soon the tired little yellow head fell off in the land of Nod.

Bert and his father were enjoying their magazines, while Mrs. Bobbsey busied herself with some fancy work, so a half-hour passed without any more excitement. At the end of that time the girls returned.

"Oh, mother!" exclaimed Nan, "we found Mrs. Manily, the matron of the Meadow Brook Fresh Air Camp, and she told us Nellie, the little cash girl, was so run down the doctors think she will have to go to the seashore. Mother, couldn't we have her down with us awhile?"

"We are only going to visit, you know, daughter, and how can we invite more company? But where is Mrs. Manily? I would like to talk to her," said Mrs. Bobbsey, who was always interested in those who worked to help the poor.

Nan and Flossie brought their mother into the next car to see the matron. We told in our book, "The Bobbsey Twins in the Country," how good a matron this Mrs. Manily was, and how little Nellie, the cash girl, one of the visitors at the Fresh Air Camp, was taken sick while there, and had to go to the hospital tent. It was this little girl that Nan wanted to have enjoy the seashore, and perhaps visit Aunt Emily.

Mrs. Manily was very glad to see Mrs. Bobbsey, for the latter had helped with money and clothing to care for the poor children at the Meadow Brook Camp.

"Why, how pleasant to meet a friend in traveling!" said the matron as she shook hands with Mrs. Bobbsey. "You are all off for the seashore, the girls tell me."

"Yes," replied Mrs. Bobbsey. "One month at the beach, and we must then hurry home to Lakeport for the school days. But Nan tells me little Nellie is not well yet?"

"No, I am afraid she will need another change of air to undo the trouble made by her close confinement in a city store. She is not seriously sick, but so run down that it will take some time for her to get strong again," said the matron.

"Have you a camp at the seashore?" asked Mrs. Bobbsey.

"No; indeed, I wish we had," answered the matron. "I am just going down now to see if I can't find some place where Nellie can stay for a few weeks."

"I'm going to visit my sister, Mrs. Minturn, at Ocean Cliff, near Sunset Beach," said Mrs. Bobbsey. "They have a large cottage and are always charitable. If they have no other company I think, perhaps, they would be glad to give poor little Nellie a room."

"That would be splendid!" exclaimed the matron. "I was going to do a line of work I never did before. I was just going to call on some of the well-to-do people, and ask them to take Nellie. We had no funds, and I felt so much depended on the change of air, I simply made up my mind to go and do what I could."

"Then you can look in at my sister's first," said Mrs. Bobbsey. "If she cannot accommodate you, perhaps she can tell who could. Now, won't you come in the other car with us, and we can finish our journey together?"

"Yes, indeed I will. Thank you," said the matron, gathering up her belongings and making her way to the Bobbsey quarters in the other car.

"Won't it be lovely to have Nellie with us!" Nan said to Flossie, as they passed along. "I am sure Aunt Emily will say yes."

"So am I," said little Flossie, whose kind heart always went out when it should. "I know surely they would not let Nellie die in the city while we enjoy the seaside."

Freddie was awake now, and also glad to see Mrs. Manily.

"Where's Sandy?" he inquired at once. Sandy had been his little chum from the Meadow Brook Camp.

"I guess he is having a nice time somewhere," replied Mrs. Manily. "His aunt found him out, you know, and is going to take care of him now."

"Well, I wish he was here too," said Freddie, rubbing his eyes. "We're goin' to have lots of fun fishing in the ocean."

The plan for Nellie was told to Mr. Bobbsey, who, of course agreed it would be very nice if Aunt Emily and Uncle William were satisfied.

"And what do you suppose those boxes contain?" said Mrs. Bobbsey to Mrs. Manily, pointing to the three boxes in the hanger above them.

"Shoes?" ventured the matron.

"Nope," said Freddie. "One hat, and my duck and my cat. Downy is my duck and Snoop is my cat."

Then Nan told about the flight of the duck and the "kidnapping" of Snoop.

"We put them up there out of the way," finished Nan, "so that nothing more can happen to them."

The afternoon was wearing out now, and the strong summer sun shrunk into thin strips through the trees, while the train dashed along. As the ocean air came in the windows, the long line of woodland melted into pretty little streams, that make their way in patches for many miles from the ocean front. "Like 'Baby Waters'" Nan said, "just growing out from the ocean, and getting a little bit bigger every year."

"Won't we soon be there?" asked Freddie, for long journeys are always tiresome, especially to a little boy accustomed to many changes in the day's play.

"One hour more," said Mr. Bobbsey, consulting his watch.

"Let's have a game of ball, Nan?" suggested Bert, who never traveled without a tennis ball in his pocket.

"How could we?" the sister inquired.

"Easily," said Bert. "We'll make up a new kind of game. We will start in the middle of the car, at the two center seats, and each move a seat away at every catch. Then, whoever misses first must go back to center again, and the one that gets to the end first, wins."

"All right," agreed Nan, who always enjoyed her twin brother's games. "We will call it Railroad Tennis."

Just as soon as Nan and Bert took their places, the other passengers became very much interested. There is such a monotony on trains that the sports the Bobbseys introduced were welcome indeed.

We do not like to seem proud, but certainly these twins did look pretty. Nan with her fine back eyes and red cheeks, and Bert just matching her; only his hair curled around, while hers fell down. Their interest in Railroad Tennis made their faces all the prettier, and no wonder the people watched them so closely.

Freddie was made umpire, to keep him out of a more active part, because he might do damage with a ball in a train, his mother said; so, as Nan and Bert passed the ball, he called,—his father prompting him:

"Ball one!"

"Ball two!"

"Ball three "

Bert jerked with a sudden jolt of the train and missed.

"Striker's out!" called the umpire, while everybody laughed because the boy had missed first.

Then Bert had to go all the way back to center, while Nan was four seats down.

Three more balls were passed, then Nan missed.

"I shouldn't have to go all the way back for the miss," protested Nan. "You went three seats back, so I'll go three back."

This was agreed to by the umpire, and the game continued.

A smooth stretch of road gave a good chance for catching, and both sister and brother kept moving toward the doors now, with three points "to the good" for Nan, as a big boy said.

Who would miss now? Everybody waited to see. The train struck a curve! Bert threw a wild ball and Nan missed it.

"Foul ball!" called the umpire, and Bert did not dispute it.

Then Nan delivered the ball.

"Oh, mercy me!" shrieked the old lady, who had thrown the handbag at Downy, the duck, "my glasses!" and there, upon the floor, lay the pieces.

Nan's ball had hit the lady right in the glasses, and it was very lucky they did not break until they came in contact with the floor.

"I'm so sorry!" Nan faltered. "The car jerked so I could not keep it."

"Never mind, my dear," answered the nice old lady, "I just enjoyed that game as much as you did, and if I hadn't stuck my eyes out so, they would not have met your ball. So, it's all right. I have another pair in my bag."

So the game ended with the accident, for it was now time to gather up the baggage for the last stop.

Night in a Barn

"Beach Junction! All off for the Junction!" called the train men, while the Bobbseys and Mrs. Manily hurried out to the small station, where numbers of carriages waited to take passengers to their cottages on the cliffs or by the sea.

"Sure we haven't forgotten anything?" asked Mrs. Bobbsey, taking a hasty inventory of the hand baggage.

"Bert's got Snoop and I've got Downy," answered Freddie, as if the animals were all that counted.

"And I've got my hatbox and flowers," added Nan.

"And I have my ferns," said little Flossie.

"I guess we're all here this time," Mr. Bobbsey finished, for nothing at all seemed to be missing.

It was almost nightfall, and the beautiful glow of an ocean sunset rested over the place. At the rear of the station an aged stage driver sat nodding on his turnout. The stage coach was an "old timer," and had carried many a merry party of sightseers through the sandy roads of Oceanport and Sunset Beach, while Hank, the driver, called out all spots of interest along the way. And Hank had a way of making things interesting.

"Pike's Peak," he would call out for Cliff Hill.

"The Giant's Causeway," he would announce for Rocky Turn.

And so Hank was a very popular stage driver, and never had to look for trade—it always came to him.

"That's our coach," said Mr. Bobbsey, espying Hank. "Hello there! Going to the beach?" he called to the sleepy driver.

"That's for you to say," replied Hank, straightening up.

"Could we get to Ocean Cliff—Minturn's place—before dark?" asked Mr. Bobbsey, noticing how rickety the old stagecoach was.

"Can't promise," answered Hank, "but you can just pile in and we'll try it." There was no choice, so the party "piled" into the carryall.

"Isn't this fun?" remarked Mrs. Manily, taking her seat up under the front window. "It's like going on a May ride."

"I'm afraid it will be a moonlight ride at this rate," laughed Mr. Bobbsey, as the stagecoach started to rattle on. Freddie wanted to sit in front with Hank but Mrs. Bobbsey thought it safer inside, for, indeed, the ride was risky enough, inside or out. As they joggled on the noise of the wheels grew louder and louder, until our friends could only make themselves heard by screaming at each other.

"Night is coming," called Mrs. Bobbsey, and Dinah said: "Suah 'nough we be out in de night dis time."

It seemed as if the old horses wanted to stand still, they moved so slowly, and the old wagon creaked and cracked until Hank, himself, turned round, looked in the window, and shouted:

"All right there?"

"Guess so," called back Mr. Bobbsey, "but we don't see the ocean yet."

"Oh, we'll get there," drawled Hank, lazily.

"We should have gone all the way by train," declared Mrs. Bobbsey, in alarm, as the stage gave one squeak louder than the others.

"Haven't you got any lanterns?" shouted Mr. Bobbsey to Hank, for it was pitch-dark now.

"Never use one," answered the driver. "When it's good and dark the moon will come up, but we'll be there 'fore that. Get 'long there, Doll!" he called to one horse. "Go 'long, Kit!" he urged the other.

The horses did move a little faster at that, then suddenly something snapped and the horses turned to one side.

"Whoa! Whoa!" called Hank, jerking on the reins. But it was too late! The stage coach was in a hole! Several screamed.

"Sit still!" called Mr. Bobbsey to the excited party. "It's only a broken shaft and the coach can't upset now."

Flossie began to cry. It was so dark and black in that hole.

Hank looked at the broken wagon.

"Well, we're done now," he announced, with as little concern as if the party had been safely landed on Aunt Emily's piazza, instead of in a hole on the roadside.

"Do you mean to say you can't fix it up?" Mr. Bobbsey almost gasped.

"Not till I get the stage to the blacksmith's," replied Hank.

"Then, what are we going to do?" Mr. Bobbsey asked, impatiently.

"Well, there's an empty barn over there," Hank answered. "The best thing you can do is pitch your tent there till I get back with another wagon."

"Barn!" exclaimed Mrs. Bobbsey.

"How long will it take you to get a wagon?" demanded Mr. Bobbsey.

"Not long," said Hank, sprucing up a trifle. "You just get yourselves comfortable in that there barn. I'll get the coach to one side, and take a horse down to Sterritt's. He'll let me have a horse and a wagon, and I'll be back as soon as I kin make it."

"There seems nothing else to do," Mr. Bobbsey said. "We may as well make the best of it."

"Why, yes," Mrs. Manily spoke up, "we can pretend we are having a barn dance." And she smiled, faintly.

Nevertheless, it was not very jolly to make their way to the barn in the dark. Dinah had to carry Freddie, he was so sleepy; Mrs. Manily took good care of Flossie. But, of course, there was the duck and the cat, that could not be very safely left in the broken-down stagecoach.

"Say, papa!" Bert exclaimed, suddenly, "I saw an old lantern up under the seat in that stagecoach. Maybe it has some oil in it. I'll go back and see."

"All right, son," replied the father, "we won't get far ahead of you." And while Bert made his way back to the wagon, the others bumped up and down through the fields that led to the vacant barn.

There was no house within sight. The barn belonged to a house up the road that the owners had not moved into that season.

"I got one!" called Bert, running up from the road. "This lantern has oil in, I can hear it rattle. Have you a match, pa?"

Mr. Bobbsey had, and when the lantern had been lighted, Bert marched on ahead of the party, swinging it in real signal fashion.

"You ought to be a brakeman," Nan told her twin brother, at which remark Bert swung his light above his head and made all sorts of funny railroad gestures.

The barn door was found unlocked, and excepting for the awful stillness about, it was not really so bad to find refuge in a good, clean place like that, for outside it was very damp—almost wet with the ocean spray. Mr. Bobbsey found seats for all, and with the big carriage doors swung open, the party sat and listened for every sound that might mean the return of the stage driver.

"Come, Freddie chile," said Dinah, "put yer head down on Dinah's lap. She won't let nothin' tech you. An' youse kin jest go to sleep if youse a mind ter. I'se a-watchin' out."

The invitation was welcome to the tired little youngster, and it was not long before he had followed Dinah's invitation.

Next, Flossie cuddled up in Mrs. Manily's arms and stopped thinking for a while.

"It is awfully lonely," whispered Nan, to her mother, "I do wish that man would come back."

"So do I," agreed the mother. "This is not a very comfortable hotel, especially as we are all tired out from a day's journey."

"What was that?" asked Bert, as a strange sound, like a howl, was heard.

"A dog," lightly answered the father.

"I don't think so," said Bert. "Listen!"

"Oh!" cried Flossie, starting up and clinging closer to Mrs. Manily, "I'm just scared to death!"

"Dinah, I want to go home," cried Freddie. "Take me right straight home."

"Hush, children, you are safe," insisted their mother. "The stage driver will be back in a few minutes."

"But what is that funny noise?" asked Freddie. "It ain't no cow, nor no dog."

The queer "Whoo-oo-oo" came louder each time. It went up and down like a scale, and "left a hole in the air," Bert declared.

"It's an owl!" exclaimed Mrs. Bobbsey, and she was right, for up in the abandoned hay loft the queer old birds had found a quiet place, and had not been disturbed before by visitors.

"Let's get after them," proposed Bert, with lantern in hand.

"You would have a queer hunt," his father told him; "I guess you had better not think of it. Hark! there's a wagon! I guess Hank is coming back to us," and the welcome sound of wheels on the road brought the party to their feet again.

"Hello there!" called Hank. "Here you are. Come along now, we'll make it this time."

It did not take the Bobbseys long to reach the roadside and there they found Hank with a big farm wagon. The seats were made of boards, and there was nothing to hold on to but the edge of the boards.

But the prospect of getting to Aunt Emily's at last made up for all their inconveniences, and when finally Hank pulled the reins again, our friends gave a sigh of relief.

A Queer Stage Driver

"I reckon I'll have to make another trip to get that old coach down to the shop," growled the stage driver, as he tried to hurry the horses, Kit and Doll, along.

"I hardly think it is worth moving," Mr. Bobbsey said, feeling somewhat indignant that a hackman should impose upon his passengers by risking their lives in such a broken-down wagon.

"Not worth it? Wall! I guess Hank don't go back on the old coach like that. Why, a little grease and a few bolts will put that rig in tip-top order." And he never made the slightest excuse for the troubles he had brought upon the Bobbseys.

"Oh, my!" cried Nan, "my hatbox! Bert you have put your foot right into my best hat!"

"Couldn't help it," answered the brother; "I either had to go through your box or go out of the back of this wagon, when that seat slipped," and he tried to adjust the board that had fallen into the wagon.

"Land sakes alive!" exclaimed Dinah. "Say, you driver man there!" she called in real earnest, "ef you doan go a little carefuler wit dis yere wagon you'll be spilling us all out. I just caught dat cat's box a-sliding, and lan' only knows how dat poor little Downy duck is, way down under dat old board."

"Hold on tight," replied Hank, as if the whole thing were a joke, and his wagon had the privilege of a toboggan slide.

"My!" sighed Mrs. Bobbsey, putting her arms closer about Flossie, "I hope nothing more happens."

"I am sure we are all right now," Mrs. Manily assured her. "The road is broad and smooth here, and it can't be far to the beach."

"Here comes a carriage," said Bert, as two pretty coach lights flashed through the trees.

"Hello there!" called someone from the carriage.

"Uncle William!" Nan almost screamed, and the next minute the carriage drew up alongside the wagon.

"Well, I declare," said Uncle William Minturn, jumping front his seat, and beginning to help the stranded party.

"We are all here," began Mr. Bobbsey, "but it was hard work to keep ourselves together."

"Oh, Uncle William," cried Freddie, "put me in your carriage. This one is breakin' down every minute."

"Come right along, my boy. I'll fix you up first," declared the uncle, giving his little nephew a good hug as he placed him on the comfortable cushions inside the big carriage.

There was not much chance for greetings as everybody was too anxious to get out of the old wagon. So, when all the boxes had been carefully put outside with the driver, and all the passengers had taken their places on the long side seats (it was one of those large side-seated carriages that Uncle William had brought, knowing he would have a big party to carry), then with a sigh of relief Mrs. Bobbsey attempted to tell something of their experiences.

"But how did you know where we were?" Bert asked.

"We had been waiting for you since four o'clock," replied Uncle William. "Then I found out that the train was late, and we waited some more. But when it came to be night and you had not arrived, I set out looking for you. I went to the Junction first, and the agent there told me you had gone in Hank's stage. I happened to be near enough to the livery stable to hear some fellows talking about Hank's breakdown, with a big party aboard. I knew then what had happened, and sent Dorothy home,—she had been out most of the afternoon waiting—got this carryall, and here we are," and Uncle William only had to hint "hurry up" to his horses and away they went.

"Oh, we did have the awfulest time," insisted Freddie.

"I feel as if we hadn't seen a house in a whole year," sighed little Flossie.

"And we only left Meadow Brook this morning," added Nan. "It does seem much longer than a day since we started."

"Well, you will be in Aunt Emily's arms in about two minutes now," declared Uncle William, as through the trees the lights from Ocean Cliff, the Minturn cottage, could now be seen.

"Hello! Hello!" called voices from the veranda.

"Aunt Emily and Dorothy!" exclaimed Bert, and called back to them:

"Here we come! Here we are!" and the wagon turned in to the broad steps at the side of the veranda.

"I've been worried to death," declared Aunt Emily, as she began kissing the girls.

"We have brought company," said Mrs. Bobbsey, introducing Mrs. Manily, "and I don't know what we should have done in all our troubles if she had not been along to cheer us up."

"We are delighted to have you," said Aunt Emily to Mrs. Manily, while they all made their way indoors.

"Oh, Nan!" cried Dorothy, hugging her cousin as tightly as ever she could, "I thought you would never come!"

"We were an awfully long time getting here," Nan answered, returning her cousin's caress, "but we had so many accidents."

"Nothing happened to your appetites, I hope," laughed Uncle William, as the dining-room doors were swung open and a table laden with good things came into sight.

"I think I could eat," said Mrs. Bobbsey, then the mechanical piano player was started, and the party made their way to the dining room.

Uncle William took Mrs. Manily to her place, as she was a stranger; Bert sat between Dorothy and Nan, Mr. Bobbsey looked after Aunt Emily, and Mr. Jack Burnet, a friend of Uncle William, who had been spending the evening at the cottage, escorted Mrs. Bobbsey to her place.

"Come, Flossie, my dear, you see I have gotten a tall chair for you," said Aunt Emily, and Flossie was made comfortable in one of those "between" chairs, higher than the others, and not as high as a baby's.

It was quite a brilliant dinner party, for the Minturns were well-to-do and enjoyed their prosperity as they went along. Mrs. Minturn had been a society belle when she was married. She was now a graceful young hostess, with a handsome husband. She had married earlier than her sister, Mrs. Bobbsey, but kept up her good times in spite of the home cares that followed. During the dinner, Dinah helped the waitress, being perhaps a little jealous that any other maid should look after the wants of Flossie and Freddie.

"Oh, Dinah!" exclaimed Freddie, as she came in with more milk for him, "did you take Snoop out of the box and did you give Downy some water?"

"I suah did, chile," said Dinah, "and you jest ought ter see that Downy duck fly 'round de kitchen. Why, he jest got one of dem fits he had on de train, and we had to shut him in de pantry to get hold ob him."

The waitress, too, told about the flying duck, and everybody enjoyed hearing about the pranks of Freddie's animals.

"We've got a lovely little pond for him, Freddie," said Dorothy. "There is a real little lake out near my donkey barn, and your duck will have a lovely time there."

"But he has to swim in the ocean," insisted Freddie, "'cause we're going to train him to be a circus duck."

"You will have to put him in a bag and tie a rope to him then," Uncle William teased, "because that's the only way a duck can swim in the ocean."

"But you don't know about Downy," argued Freddie. "He's wonderful! He even tried to swim without any water, on the train."

"Through the looking glass!" said Bert, laughing.

"And through the air," added Nan.

"I tell you, Freddie," said Uncle William, quite seriously: "we could get an airship for him maybe; then he could really swim without water."

But Freddie took no notice of the way they tried to make fun of his duck, for he felt Downy was really wonderful, as he said, and would do some wonderful things as soon as it got a chance.

When dinner was over, Dorothy took Nan up to her room. On the dresser, in a cut-glass bowl, were little Nettie Prentice's lilies that Nan had carried all the way from Meadow Brook, and they were freshened up beautifully, thanks to Dorothy's thoughtfulness in giving them a cold spray in the bath tub.

"What a lovely room!" Nan exclaimed, in unconcealed admiration.

"Do you like it?" said Dorothy. "It has a lovely view of the ocean and I chose it for you because I know you like to see pretty sights out of your window. The sun seems to rise just under this window," and she brushed aside the dainty curtains.

The moonlight made a bright path out on the ocean and Nan stood looking out, spellbound.

"I think the ocean is so grand," she said. "It always makes me feel so small and helpless."

"When you are under a big wave," laughed her cousin, who had a way of being jolly. "I felt that way the other day. Just see my arm," and Dorothy pushed up her short sleeve, displaying a black and blue bruise too high up to be seen except in an evening dress or bathing costume.

"How did you do that?" asked Nan, in sympathy.

"Ran into a pier," returned the cousin, with unconcern. "I thought my arm was broken first. But we must go down," said Dorothy, while Nan wanted to see all the things in her pretty room. "We always sit outside before retiring. Mamma says the ocean sings a lullaby that cures all sorts of bad dreams and sleeplessness."

On the veranda Nan and Dorothy joined the others. Freddie was almost asleep in Aunt Emily's arms; Uncle William, Mr. Bobbsey, and Mr. Burnet were talking, with Bert as an interested listener; while Mrs. Manily told Aunt Emily of her mission to the beach. As the children had thought, Aunt Emily readily gave consent to have Nellie, the little cash girl, come to Ocean Cliff, and on the morrow Nan and Dorothy were to write the letter of invitation.

The Ocean

Is there anything more beautiful than sunrise on the ocean?

Nan crept out of bed at the first peep of dawn, and still in her white robe, she sat in the low window seat to see the sun rise "under her window."

"What a beautiful place!" Nan thought, when dawn gave her a chance to see Ocean Cliff. "Dorothy must be awfully happy here. To see the ocean from a bedroom window!" and she watched the streaks of dawn make maps on the waves. "If I were a writer I would always put the ocean in my book," she told herself, "for there are so many children who never have a chance to see the wonderful world of water!"

Nettie's flowers were still on the dresser.

"Poor little Nettie Prentice," thought Nan. "She has never seen the ocean and I wonder if she ever will!"

Nan touched the lilies reverently. There was something in the stillness of daybreak that made the girl's heart go out to poor Nettie, just like the timid little sunbeams went out over the waters, trying to do their small part in lighting up a day.

"I'll just put the lilies out in the dew," Nan went on to herself, raising the window quietly, for the household was yet asleep. "Perhaps I'll find someone sick or lonely to-morrow who will like them, and it will be so much better if they bring joy to someone, for they are so sweet and pretty to die just for me."

"Oh!" screamed Nan the next minute, for someone had crept up behind her and covered her eyes with hands. "It is you, Dorothy!" she declared, getting hold of the small fingers. "Did I wake you with the window?"

"Yes, indeed, I thought someone was getting in from the piazza. They always come near morning," said Dorothy, dropping down on the cushions of the window seat like a goddess of morn, for Dorothy was a beautiful girl, all pink and gold, Bert said, excepting for her eyes, and they were like Meadow Brook violets, deep blue. "Did you have the nightmare?" she asked.

"Nightmare, indeed!" Nan exclaimed. "Why, you told me the sun would rise under my window and I got up to—"

"See it do the rise!" laughed Dorothy, in her jolly way. "Well, if I had my say I'd make Mr. Sol-Sun wear a mask and keep his glare to himself until respectable people felt like crawling out. I lower my awning and close the inside blinds every night. I like sunshine in reasonable doses at reasonable hours, but the moon is good enough for me in the meantime," and she fell over in a pretty lump, feigning sleep in Nan's cushions.

"I hope I did not wake anyone else," said Nan.

"Makes no difference about me, of course," laughed the jolly Dorothy. "Well, I'll pay you back, Nan. Be careful. I am bound to get even," and Nan knew that some trick was in store for her, as Dorothy had the reputation of being full of fun, and always playing tricks.

The sun was up in real earnest now, and the girls raised the window sash to let in the soft morning air.

"I think this would really cure Nellie, my little city friend," said Nan, "and you don't know what a nice girl she is."

"Just bring her down and I'll find out all about her," said Dorothy. "I love city girls. They are so wide awake, and never say silly things like—like some girls I know," she finished, giving her own cousin a good hug that belied the attempt at making fun of her.

"Nellie is sensible," Nan said, "and yet she knows how to laugh, too. She said she had never been in a carriage until she had a ride with us at Meadow Brook. Think of that!"

"Wait till she sees my donkeys!" Dorothy finished, gathering herself up from the cushions and preparing to leave. "Well, Nannie dear, I have had a lovely time," and she made a mock social bow. "Come to see me some time and have some of my dawn, only don't come before eleven A.M. or you might get mixed up, for its awful dark in the blue room until that hour." And like a real fairy Dorothy shook her golden hair and, stooping low in myth fashion, made a "bee-line" across the hall.

"She doesn't need any brother," Nan thought as she saw Dorothy bolt in her door like a squirrel; "she is so jolly and funny!"

But the girls were not the only ones who arose early that morning, for Bert and his father came in to breakfast from a walk on the sands.

"It's better than Meadow Brook," Bert told Nan, as she took her place at the table. "I wish Harry would come down."

"It is so pleasant we want all our friends to enjoy it," said Mrs. Bobbsey. "But I'm sure you have quite a hotel full now, haven't you, Dorothy?"

"Lots more rooms up near the roof," replied Dorothy, "and it's a pity to waste them when there's plenty of ocean to spare. Now, Freddie," went on Dorothy, "when we finish breakfast I am going to show you my donkeys. I called one Doodle and the other Dandy, because papa gave them to me on Decoration Day."

"Why didn't you call one Uncle Sam?" asked Freddie, remembering his part in the Meadow Brook parade.

"Well, I thought Doodle Dandy was near enough red, white, and blue," said Dorothy.

The children finished breakfast rather suddenly and then made their way to the donkey barn.

"Oh, aren't they lovely!" exclaimed Nan, patting the pretty gray animals. "I think they are prettier than horses, they are not so tall."

"I know all about goats and donkeys," declared Freddie.

"I know Nan likes everything early, so we will give her an early ride," proposed Dorothy.

The Bobbseys watched their cousin with interest as she fastened all the bright buckles and put the straps together, harnessing the donkeys. Bert helped so readily that he declared he would do all the harnessing thereafter. The cart was one of those pretty, little basket affairs, with seats at the side, and Bert was very proud of being able to drive a team. There were Dorothy, Nan, Freddie, Flossie, and Bert in the cart when they rode along the sandy driveway, and they made a very pretty party in their bright summer costumes. Freddie had hold of Doodle's reins, and he insisted that his horse went along better than did Dandy, on the other side.

"Oh, won't Nellie enjoy this!" cried Nan, thinking of the little city girl who had only had one carriage ride in all her life.

"Mrs. Manily is going up to the city to bring her to-day," said Bert. "Aunt Emily sent for the depot wagon just as we came out."

Like many people at the seashore, the Minturns did not keep their own horses, but simply had to telephone from their house to the livery stable when they wanted a carriage.

"Oh, I see the ocean!" called out Freddie, as Bert drove nearer the noise of the waves. "Why didn't we bring Downy for his swim?"

"Too early to bathe yet!" said Dorothy. "We have a bathing house all to ourselves,—papa rented it for the summer,—and about eleven o'clock we will come down and take a dip. Mamma always comes with me or sends Susan, our maid. Mamma cannot believe I really know how to swim."

"And do you?" asked Nan, in surprise.

"Wait until you see!" replied the cousin. "And I am going to teach you, too."

"I'd love to know how, but it must be awfully hard to learn," answered Nan.

"Not a bit," went on Dorothy; "I learned in one week. We have a pool just over there, and lots of girls are learning every day. You can drive right along the beach, Bert; the donkeys are much safer than horses and never attempt to run away."

How delightful it was to ride so close to the great rolling ocean! Even Freddie stopped exclaiming, and just watched the waves, as one after another they tried to get right under Dorothy's cart.

"It makes me almost afraid!" faltered little Flossie, as the great big waves came up so high out on the waters, they seemed like mountains that would surely cover up the donkey cart. But when they "broke" on the sands they were only little splashy puddles for babies to wash their pink toes in.

"There's Blanche Bowden," said Dorothy, as another little cart, a pony cart, came along. "We have lovely times together. I have invited her up to meet us this afternoon, Nan."

The other girl bowed pleasantly from her cart, and even Freddie remembered to raise his cap, something he did not always think necessary for "just girls."

"Some afternoon our dancing class is going to have a matinee," said Dorothy. "Do you like dancing, Bert?"

"Some," replied her cousin in a boy's indifferent way. "Nan is a good dancer."

"Oh, we don't have real dances," protested Nan; "they are mostly drills and exercises. Mamma doesn't believe in young children going right into society. She thinks we will be old soon enough."

"We don't have grown-up dances," said Dorothy, "only the two-step and minuet. I think the minuet is the prettiest of all dances."

"We have had the varsovienne," said Nan, "that is like the minuet. Mother says they are old-time dances, but they are new in our class."

"We may have a costume affair next month," went on Dorothy. "Some of the girls want it, but I don't like wigs and long dresses, especially for dancing. I get all tangled up in a train dress."

"I never wore one," said Nan, "excepting at play, and I can't see how any girl can dance with a lot of long skirts dangling around."

"Oh, they mostly bow and smile," put in Bert, "and a boy has to be awfully careful at one of those affairs. If he should step on a skirt there surely would be trouble," and he snapped his whip at the donkeys with the air of one who had little regard for the graceful art of dancing.

"We had better go back now," said Dorothy, presently. "You haven't had a chance to see our own place yet, but I thought you wanted to get acquainted with the ocean first. Everybody does!"

"I have enjoyed it so much!" declared Nan. "It is pleasanter now than when the sun grows hot."

"But we need the sun for bathing," Dorothy told her. "That is why we 'go in' at the noon hour."

The drive back to the Cliff seemed very short, and when the children drove up to the side porch they found Mrs. Bobbsey and Aunt Emily sitting outside with their fancy work.

Freddie could hardly find words to tell his mother how big the ocean was, and Flossie declared the water ran right into the sky it was so high.

"Now, girls," said Aunt Emily, "Mrs. Manily has gone to bring Nellie down, so you must go and arrange her room. I think the front room over Nan's will be best. Now get out all your pretty things, Dorothy, for little Nellie may be lonely and want some things to look at."

"All right, mother," answered Dorothy, letting Bert put the donkeys away, "we'll make her room look like—like a valentine," she finished, always getting some fun in even where very serious matters were concerned.

The two girls, with Flossie looking on, were soon very busy with Nellie's room.

"We must not make it too fussy," said Dorothy, "or Nellie may not feel at home; and we certainly want her to enjoy herself. Will we put a pink or blue set on the dresser?"

"Blue," said Nan, "for I know she loves blue. She said so when we picked violets at Meadow Brook."

"All right," agreed Dorothy. "And say! Let's fix up something funny! We'll get all the alarm clocks in the house and set them so they will go off one after the other, just when Nellie gets to bed, say about nine o'clock. We'll hide them so she will just about find one when the other starts! She isn't really sick, is she?" Dorothy asked, suddenly remembering that the visitor might not be in as good spirits as she herself was.

"Oh, no, only run down," answered Nan, "and I'm sure she would enjoy the joke."

So the girls went on fixing up the pretty little room. Nan ran downstairs and brought up Nettie Prentice's flowers.

"I thought they would do someone good," she said. "They are so fragrant."

"Aren't they!" Dorothy said, burying her pretty nose in the white lilies. "They smell better than florists' bouquets. I suppose that's from the country air. Now I'll go collect clocks," and without asking anyone's permission Dorothy went from room to room, snatching alarm clocks from every dresser that held one.

"Susan's is a peach," she told Nan, apologizing with a smile, for the slang. "It goes off for fifteen minutes if you don't stop it, and it sounds like a church bell."

"Nellie will think she has gotten into college," Nan said, laughing. "This is like hazing, isn't it?"

"Only we won't really annoy her," said Dorothy. "We just want to make her laugh. College boys, they say, do all sorts of mean things. Make a boy swim in an icy river and all that."

"I hope Bert never goes to a school where they do hazing," said Nan, feeling for her brother's safety. "I think such sport is just wicked!"

"So do I," declared Dorothy, "and if I were a new fellow, and they played such tricks on me, I would just wait for years if I had to, to pay them back."

"I'd put medicine in their coffee, or do something."

"They ought to be arrested," Nan said, "and if the professors can't stop it they should not be allowed to run such schools."

"There," said Dorothy, "I guess everything is all right for Nellie." She put a rose jar on a table in the alcove window. "Now I'll wind the clocks. You mustn't look where I put them," and she insisted that not even Nan should know the mystery of the clocks. "This will be a real surprise party," finished Dorothy, having put each of five clocks in its hiding place, and leaving the tick-ticks to think it over, all by themselves, before going off.

Nellie

"Shall I take my cart over to meet Nellie and Mrs. Manily, mother?" Dorothy asked Mrs. Minturn, that afternoon, when the city train was about due.

"Why, yes, daughter, I think that would be very nice," replied the mother. "I intended to send the depot wagon, but the cart would be very enjoyable."

Bert had the donkeys hitched up and at the door for Nan and Dorothy in a very few minutes, and within a half-hour from that time Nan was greeting Nellie at the station, and making her acquainted with Dorothy.

If Dorothy had expected to find in the little cash girl a poor, sickly, ill child, she must have been disappointed, for the girl that came with Mrs. Manily had none of these failings. She was tall and graceful, very pale, but nicely dressed, thanks to Mrs. Manily's attention after she reached the city on the morning train. With a gift from Mrs. Bobbsey, Nellie was "fitted up from head to foot," and now looked quite as refined a little girl as might be met anywhere.

"You were so kind to invite me!" Nellie said to Dorothy, as she took her seat in the cart. "This is such a lovely place!" and she nodded toward the wonderful ocean, without giving a hint that she had never before seen it.

"Yes, you are sure the air is so strong you must swallow strength all the time," and Nellie knew from the remark that Dorothy was a jolly girl, and would not talk sickness, like the people who visit poor children at hospital tents.

Even Mrs. Manily, who knew Nellie to be a capable girl, was surprised at the way she "fell in" with Nan and Dorothy, and Mrs. Manily was quite charmed with her quiet, reserved manner. The fact was that Nellie had met so many strangers in the big department store, she was entirely at ease and accustomed to the little polite sayings of people in the fashionable world.

When Nellie unpacked her bag she brought out something for Freddie. It was a little milk wagon, with real cans, which Freddie could fill up with "milk" and deliver to customers.

"That is to make you think of Meadow Brook," said Nellie, when she gave him the little wagon.

"Yes, and when there's a fire," answered Freddie, "I can fill the cans with water and dump it on the fire like they do in Meadow Brook, too." Freddie always insisted on being a fireman and had a great idea of putting fires out and climbing ladders.

There was still an hour to spare before dinner, and Nan proposed that they take a walk down to the beach. Nellie went along, of course, but when they got to the great stretch of white sand, near the waves, the girls noticed Nellie was about to cry.

"Maybe she is too tired," Nan whispered to Dorothy, as they made some excuse to go back home again. All along the way Nellie was very quiet, almost in tears, and the other girls were disappointed, for they had expected her to enjoy the ocean so much. As soon as they reached home Nellie went to her room, and Nan and Dorothy told Mrs. Minturn about their friend's sudden sadness. Mrs. Minturn of course, went up to see if she could do anything for Nellie.

There she found the little stranger crying as if her heart would break.

"Oh, I can't help it, Mrs. Minturn!" she sobbed. "It was the ocean. Father must be somewhere in that big, wild sea!" and again she cried almost hysterically.

"Tell me about it, dear," said Mrs. Minturn, with her arm around the child. "Was your father drowned at sea?"

"Oh no; that is, we hope he wasn't." said Nellie, through her tears, "but sometimes we feel he must be dead or he would write to poor mother."

"Now dry your tears, dear, or you will have a headache," said Mrs. Minturn, and Nellie soon recovered her composure.

"You see," she began, "we had such a nice home and father was always so good. But a man came and asked him to go to sea. The man said they would make lots of money in a short time. This man was a great friend of father and he said he needed someone he could trust on this voyage. First father said no, but when he talked it over with mother, they, thought it would be best to go, if they could get so much money in a short time, so he went."

Here Nellie stopped again and her dark eyes tried hard to keep back the tears.

"When was that?" Mrs. Minturn asked.

"A year ago," Nellie replied, "and he was only to be away six months at the most."

"And that was why you had to leave school, wasn't it?" Mrs. Minturn questioned further.

"Yes, we had not much money saved, and mother got sick from worrying, so I did not mind going to work. I'm going back to the store again as soon as the doctor says I can," and the little girl showed how anxious she was to help her mother.

"But your father may come back," said Mrs. Minturn; "sailors are often out drifting about for months, and come in finally. I would not be discouraged—you cannot tell what day your father may come back with all the money, and even more than he expected."

"Oh, I know," said Nellie. "I won't feel like that again. It was only because it was the first time I saw the ocean. I'm never homesick or blue. I don't believe in making people pity you all the time." And the brave little girl jumped up, dried her eyes, and looked as if she would never cry again as long as she lived—like one who had cried it out and done with it.

"Yes, you must have a good time with the girls," said Mrs. Minturn. "I guess you need fun more than any medicine."

That evening at dinner Nellie was her bright happy self again, and the three girls chatted merrily about all the good times they would have at the seashore.

There was a ride to the depot after dinner, for Mrs. Manily insisted that she had to leave for the city that evening, and after a game of ball on the lawn, in which everybody, even Flossie and Freddie, had a hand, the children prepared to retire. There was to be a shell hunt very early in the morning (that was a long walk on the beach, looking for choice shells), so the girls wanted to go to bed an hour before the usual time.

"Wait till the clock strikes, Nellie," sang Dorothy, as they went upstairs, and, of course, no one but Nan knew what she meant.

Two hours after this the house was all quiet, when suddenly, there was the buzz of an alarm clock.

"What was that?" asked Mrs. Minturn, coming out in the hall.

"An alarm clock," called Nellie, in whose room the disturbance was. "I found it under my pillow," she added innocently, never suspecting that Dorothy had put it there purposely.

By and by everything was quiet again, when another gong went off.

"Well, I declare!" said Mrs. Minturn. "I do believe Dorothy has been up to some pranks."

"*Ding—a-ling—a-long—a-ling!*" went the clock, and Nellie was laughing outright, as she searched about the room for the newest alarm. She had a good hunt, too, for the clock was in the shoe box in the farthest corner of the room.

After that there was quite an intermission, as Dorothy expressed it. Even Nellie had stopped laughing and felt very sleepy, when another clock started.

This was the big gong that belonged in Susan's room, and at the sound of it Freddie rushed out in the hall, yelling.

"That's a fire bell! Fire! fire! fire!" he shouted, while everybody else came out this time to investigate the disturbance.

"Now, Dorothy!" said Mrs. Minturn, "I know you have done this. Where did you put those clocks?"

Dorothy only laughed in reply, for the big bell was ringing furiously all the time. Nellie had her dressing robe on, and opened the door to those outside her room.

"I guess it's ghosts," she laughed. "They are all over."

"A serenade," called Bert, from his door.

"What ails dem der clocks?" shouted Dinah. "'Pears like as if dey had a fit, suah. Nebber heard such clockin' since we was in de country," and Susan, who had discovered the loss of her clock, laughed heartily, knowing very well who had taken the alarm away.

When the fifteen minutes were up that clock stopped, and another started. Then there was a regularly cannonading, Bert said, for there was scarcely a moment's quiet until every one of the six clocks had gone off "bing, bang, biff," as Freddie said.

There was no use trying to locate them, for they went off so rapidly that Nellie knew they would go until they were "all done," so she just sat down and waited.

"Think you'll wake up in time?" asked Dorothy, full of mischief as she came into the clock corner.

"I guess so," Nellie answered, laughing. "We surely were alarmed to-night." Then aside to Nan, Nellie whispered: "Wait, we'll get even with her, won't we?" And Nan nodded with a sparkle in her eyes.

Exploring—a Race for Pond Lilies

"Now let's explore," Bert said to the girls the next morning. "We haven't had a chance yet to see the lake, the woods, or the island."

"Hal Bingham is coming over to see you this morning," Dorothy told Bert. "He said you must be tired toting girls around, and he knows everything interesting around here to show you."

"Glad of it," said Bert. "You girls are very nice, of course, but a boy needs another fellow in a place like this," and he swung himself over the rail of the veranda, instead of walking down the steps.

It was quite early, for there was so much planned, to be accomplished before the sun got too hot, that all the children kept to their promise to get up early, and be ready for the day's fun by seven o'clock. The girls, with Mrs. Bobbsey, Mrs. Minturn, and Freddie, were to go shell hunting, but as Bert had taken that trip with his father on the first morning after their arrival, he preferred to look over the woods and lake at the back of the Minturn home, where the land slid down from the rough cliff upon which the house stood.

"Here comes Hal now," called Dorothy, as a boy came whistling up the path. He was taller than Bert, but not much older, and he had a very "jolly squint" in his black eyes; that is, Dorothy called it a "jolly squint," but other people said it was merely a twinkle. But all agreed that Hal was a real boy, the greatest compliment that could be paid him.

There was not much need of an introduction, although Dorothy did call down from the porch, "Bert that's Hal; Hal that's Bert," to which announcement the boys called back, "All right, Dorothy. We'll get along."

"Have you been on the lake yet?" Hal asked, as they started down the green stretch that bounded the pretty lake on one side, while a strip of woodland pressed close to the edge across the sheet of water.

"No," Bert answered, "we have had so much coming and going to the depot since we came down, I couldn't get a chance to look around much. It's an awfully pretty lake, isn't it?"

"Yes, and it runs in and out for miles," Hal replied. "I have a canoe down here at our boathouse. Let's take a sail."

The Bingham property, like the Minturn, was on a cliff at the front, and ran back to the lake, where the little boathouse was situated. The house was made of cedars, bound together in rustic fashion, and had comfortable seats inside for ladies to keep out of the sun while waiting for a sail.

"Father and I built this house," Hal told Bert. "We were waiting so long for the carpenters, we finally got a man to bring these cedars in from Oakland. Then we had him cut them, that is, the line of uprights, and we built the boathouse without any trouble at all. It was sport to arrange all the little turns and twists, like building a block house in the nursery."

"You certainly made a good job of it," said Bert, looking critically over the boathouse.

"It's all in the design, of course; the nailing together is the easiest part."

"You might think so," said Hal, "but it's hard to drive a nail in round cedar. But we thought it so interesting, we didn't mind the trouble," finished Hal, as he prepared to untie his canoe.

"What a pretty boat!" exclaimed Bert, in real admiration.

The canoe was green and brown, the body being colored like bark, while inside, the lining was of pale green. The name, *Dorothy*, shone in rustic letters just above the water edge.

"And you called it *Dorothy*," Bert remarked.

"Yes, she's the liveliest girl I know, and a good friend of mine all summer," said Hal. "There are some boys down the avenue, but they don't know as much about good times as Dorothy does. Why, she can swim, row, paddle, climb trees, and goes in for almost any sport that's on. Last week she swam so far in the sun she couldn't touch an oar or paddle for days, her arms were so blistered. But she didn't go around with her hands in a muff at that. Dorothy's all right," finished Hal.

Bert liked to hear his cousin complimented, especially when he had such admiration himself for the girl who never pouted, and he knew that the tribute did not in any way take from Dorothy's other good quality, that of being a refined and cultured girl.

"Girls don't have to be babies to be ladylike," added Bert. "Nan always plays ball with me, and can skate and all that. She's not afraid of a snowball, either."

"Well, I'm all alone," said Hal. "Haven't even got a first cousin. We've been coming down here since I was a youngster, so that's why Dorothy seems like my sister. We used to make mud pies together."

The boys were in the canoe now, and each took a paddle. The water was so smooth that the paddles merely patted it, like "brushing a cat's back," Bert said, and soon the little bark was gliding along down the lake, in and out of the turns, until the "narrows" were reached.

"Here's where we get our pond lilies," said Hal.

"Oh, let's get some!" exclaimed Bert. "Mother is so fond of them."

It was not difficult to gather the beautiful blooms, that nested so cosily on the cool waters, too fond of their cradle to ever want to creep, or walk upon their slender green limbs. They just rocked there, with every tiny ripple of the water, and only woke up to see the warm sunlight bleaching their dainty, yellow heads.

"Aren't they fragrant?" said Bert, as he put one after the other into the bottom of the canoe.

"There's nothing like them," declared Hal. "Some people like roses best, but give me the pretty pond lilies," he finished.

The morning passed quickly, for there was so much to see around the lake. Wild ducks tried to find out how near they could go to the water without touching it, and occasionally one would splash in, by accident.

"What large birds there are around the sea," Bert remarked. "I suppose they have to be big and strong to stand long trips without food when the waves are very rough and they can hardly see fish."

"Yes, and they have such fine plumage," said Hal. "I've seen birds around here just like those in museums, all colors, and with all kinds of feathers—Birds of Paradise, I guess they call them."

"Do you ever go shooting?"

"No, not in summer time," replied Hal. "But sometimes father and I take a run down here about Thanksgiving. That's the time for seaside sport. Why, last year we fished with rakes; just raked the fish up in piles—'frosties,' they call them."

"That must be fun," reflected Bert.

"Maybe you could come this year," continued Hal. "We might make up a party, if you have school vacation for a week. We could camp out in our house, and get our meals at the hotel."

"That would be fine!" exclaimed Bert. "Maybe Uncle William would come, and perhaps my Cousin Harry, from Meadow Brook. He loves that sort of sport. By the way, we expect him down for a few days; perhaps next week."

"Good!" cried Hal. "The boat carnival is on next week. I'm sure he would enjoy that."

The boys were back at the boathouse now, and Bert gathered up his pond lilies.

"There'll be a scramble for them when the girls see them," he said. "Nellie McLaughlin, next to Dorothy, is out for fun. She is not a bit like a sick girl."

"Perhaps she isn't sick now," said Hal, "but has to be careful. She seems quite thin."

"Mother says she wants fun, more than medicine," went on Bert. "I guess she had to go to work because her father is away at sea. He's been gone a year and he only expected to be away six months."

"So is my Uncle George," remarked Hal. "He went to the West Indies to bring back a valuable cargo of wood. He had only a small vessel, and a few men. Say, did you say her name was McLaughlin?" exclaimed Hal, suddenly.

"Yes; they call him Mack for short, but his name is McLaughlin."

"Why, that was the name of the man who went with Uncle George!" declared Hal. "Maybe it was her father."

"Sounds like it," Bert said. "Tell Uncle William about it sometime. I wouldn't mention it to Nellie, she cut up so, they said, the first time she saw the ocean. Poor thing! I suppose she just imagined her father was tossing about in the waves."

The boys had tied the canoe to its post, and now made their way up over the hill toward the house.

"Here they come," said Bert, as Nan, Nellie, and Dorothy came racing down the hill.

"Oh!" cried Dorothy, "give me some!"

"Oh, you know me, Bert?" pleaded Nellie.

"Hal, I wound up your kite string, didn't I?" insisted Nan, by way of showing that she surely deserved some of Hal's pond lilies.

"And I found your ball in the bushes, Bert," urged Dorothy.

"They're not for little girls," Hal said, waving his hand comically, like a duke in a comic opera. "Run along, little girls, run along," he said, rolling his r's in real stage fashion, and holding the pond lilies against his heart.

"But if we get them, may we have them sir knight?" asked Dorothy, keeping up the joke.

"You surely can!" replied Hal, running short on his stage words.

At this Nellie dashed into the path ahead of Hal, and Dorothy turned toward Bert. Nan crowded in close to Dorothy, and the boys had some dodging to get a start. Finally Hal shot out back of the big bush, and Nellie darted after him. Of course, the boys were better runners than the girls, but somehow, girls always expect something wonderful to happen, when they start on a race like that. Hal had tennis slippers on, and he went like a deer. But just as he was about to call "home free" and as he reached the donkey barn, he turned on his ankle.

Nellie had her hands on the pond lilies instantly, for Hal was obliged to stop and nurse his ankle.

"They're yours," he gave in, handing her the beautiful bunch of blooms.

"Oh, aren't they lovely!" exclaimed the little cash girl, but no one knew that was the first time she ever, in all her life, held a pond lily in her hand.

"I'm going to give them to Mrs. Bobbsey," she decided, starting at once to the house with the fragrant prize in her arms. Neither Dorothy nor Nan had caught Bert, but he handed his flowers to his cousin.

"Give them to Aunt Emily," he said gallantly, while Dorothy took the bouquet and declared she could have caught Bert, anyhow, if she "only had a few more feet," whatever that meant.

Fun on the Sands

"How many shells did you get in your hunt?" Bert asked the girls, when the excitement over the pond lilies had died away.

"We never went," replied Dorothy. "First, Freddie fell down and had to cry awhile, then he had to stop to see the gutter band, next he had a ride on the five-cent donkey, and by that time there were so many people out, mother said there would not be a pretty shell left, so we decided to go to-morrow morning."

"Then Hal and I will go along," said Bert. "I want to look for nets, to put in my den at home."

"We are going for a swim now," went on Dorothy; "we only came back for our suits."

"There seems so much to do down here, it will take a week to have a try at everything," said Bert. "I've only been in the water once, but I'm going for a good swim now. Come along, Hal."

"Yes, we always go before lunch," said Hal starting off for his suit.

Soon Dorothy, Nan, Nellie, and Flossie appeared with their suits done up in the neat little rubber bags that Aunt Emily had bought at a hospital fair. Then Freddie came with Mrs. Bobbsey, and Dorothy, with her bag on a stick over her shoulder, led the procession to the beach.

As Dorothy told Nan, they had a comfortable bathhouse rented for the season, with plenty of hooks to hang things on, besides a mirror, to see how one's hair looked, after the waves had done it up mermaid fashion.

It did not take the girls long to get ready, and presently all appeared on the beach in pretty blue and white suits, with the large white sailor collars, that always make bathing suits look just right, because real sailors wear that shape of collar.

Flossie wore a white flannel suit, and with her pretty yellow curls, she "looked like a doll," so Nellie said. Freddie's suit was white too, as he always had things as near like his twin sister's as a boy's clothes could be. Altogether the party made a pretty summer picture, as they ran down to the waves, and promptly dipped in.

"Put your head under or you'll take cold," called Dorothy, as she emerged from a big wave that had completely covered her up.

Nellie and Nan "ducked" under, but Flossie was a little timid, and held her mother's right hand even tighter than Freddie clung to her left.

"We must get hold of the ropes," declared Mrs. Bobbsey, seeing a big wave coming.

They just reached the ropes when the wave caught them. Nellie and Nan were out farther, and the billow struck Nellie with such force it actually washed her up on shore.

"Ha! ha!" laughed Dorothy, "Nellie got the first tumble." And then the waves kept dashing in so quickly that there was no more chance for conversation. Freddie ducked under as every wave came, but Flossie was not always quick enough, and it was very hard for her to keep hold of the ropes when a big splasher dashed against her. Dorothy had not permission to swim out as far as she wanted to go, for her mother did not allow her outside the lines, excepting when Mr. Minturn was swimming near her, so she had to be content with floating around near where the other girls bounced up and down, like the bubbles on the billows.

"Look out, Nan!" called Dorothy, suddenly, as Nan stood for a moment fixing her belt. But the warning came too late, for the next minute a wave picked Nan up and tossed her with such force against a pier, that everybody thought she must be hurt. Mrs. Bobbsey was quite frightened, and ran out on the beach, putting Freddie and Flossie at a safe distance from the water, while she made her way to where Nan had been tossed.

For a minute or so, it seemed, Nan disappeared, but presently she bobbed up, out of breath, but laughing, for Hal had her by the hand, and was helping her to shore. The boys had been swimming around by themselves near by, and Hal saw the wave making for Nan just in time to get there first.

"I had to swim that time," laughed Nan, "whether I knew how or not."

"You made a pretty good attempt," Hal told her; "and the water is very deep around those piles. You had better not go out so far again, until you've learned a few strokes in the pools. Get Dorothy to teach you."

"Oh, oh, oh, Nellie!" screamed Mrs. Bobbsey. "Where is she? She has gone under that wave!"

Sure enough, Nellie had disappeared. She had only let go the ropes one minute, but she had her back to the ocean watching Nan's rescue, when a big billow struck her, knocked her down, and then where was she?

"Oh," cried Freddie. "She is surely drowned!"

Hal struck out toward where Nellie had been last seen, but he had only gone a few strokes when Bert appeared with Nellie under his arm. She had received just the same kind of toss Nan got, and fortunately Bert was just as near by to save her, as Hal had been to save Nan. Nellie, too, was laughing and out of breath when Bert towed her in.

"I felt like a rubber ball," she said, as soon as she could speak, "and Bert caught me on the first bounce."

"You girls should have ropes around your waists, and get someone to hold the other end," teased Dorothy, coming out with the others on the sands.

"Well, I think we have all had enough of the water for this morning," said Mrs. Bobbsey, too nervous to let the girls go in again.

Boys and girls were willing to take a sun bath on the beach, so, while Hal and Bert started in to build a sand house for Freddie, the four girls capered around, playing tag and enjoying themselves generally. Flossie thought it great fun to dig for the little soft crabs that hide in the deep damp sand. She found a pasteboard box and into this she put all her fish.

"I've got a whole dozen!" she called to Freddie, presently. But Freddie was so busy with his sand castle he didn't have time to bother with baby crabs.

"Look at our fort," called Bert to the girls. "We can shoot right through our battlements," he declared, as he sank down in the sand and looked out through the holes in the sand fort.

"Shoot the Indian and you get a cigar," called Dorothy, taking her place as "Indian" in front of the fort, and playing target for the boys.

First Hal tossed a pebble through a window in the fort, then Bert tried it, but neither stone went anywhere near Dorothy, the "Indian."

"Now, my turn," she claimed, squatting down back of the sand wall and taking aim at Hal, who stood out front.

And if she didn't hit him—just on the foot with a little white pebble!

"Hurrah for our sharpshooter!" cried Bert.

Of course the hard part of the trick was to toss a pebble through the window without knocking down the wall, but Dorothy stood to one side, and swung her arm, so that the stone went straight through and reached Hal, who stood ten feet away.

"I'm next," said Nellie, taking her place behind "the guns."

Nellie swung her arm and down came the fort!

"Oh my!" called Freddie, "you've knocked down the whole gun wall. You'll have to be—"

"Court-martialed," said Hal, helping Freddie out with his war terms.

"She's a prisoner of war," announced Bert, getting hold of Nellie, who dropped her head and acted like someone in real distress. Just as if it were all true, Nan and Dorothy stood by, wringing their hands, in horror, while the boys brought the poor prisoner to the frontier, bound her hands with a piece of cord, and stood her up against an abandoned umbrella pole.

Hal acted as judge.

"Have you anything to say why sentence should not be pronounced upon you?" he asked in a severe voice.

"I have," sighed Nellie. "I did not intend to betray my country. The enemy caused the—the—downfall of Quebec," she stammered, just because the name of that place happened to come to her lips.

"Who is her counsel?" asked the Judge.

"Your honor," spoke up Dorothy, "this soldier has done good service. She has pegged stones at your honor with good effect, she has even captured a company of wild pond lilies in your very ranks, and now, your honor, I plead for mercy."

The play of the children had, by this time, attracted quite a crowd, for the bathing hour was over, and idlers tarried about.

"Fair play!" called a strange boy in the crowd, taking up the spirit of fun. "That soldier has done good service. She took a sassy little crab out of my ear this very day!"

Freddie looked on as if it were all true. Flossie did not laugh a bit, but really seemed quite frightened.

"I move that sentence be pronounced," called Bert, being on the side of the prosecution.

"The prisoner will look this way!" commanded Hal.

Nellie tossed back her wet brown curls and faced the crowd.

"The sentence of the court is that the prisoner be transported for life," announced Hal, while four boys fell in around Nellie, and she silently marched in military fashion toward the bathing pavilion, with Dorothy and Nan at her heels.

Here the war game ended, and everyone was satisfied with that day's fun on the sands.

The Shell Hunt

"Now, all ready for the hunting expedition," called Uncle William, very early the next morning, he having taken a day away from his office in the city, to enjoy himself with the Bobbseys at the seashore.

It was to be a long journey, so Aunt Emily thought it wise to take the donkey cart, so that the weary travelers, as they fell by the wayside, might be put in the cart until refreshed. Besides, the shells and things could be brought home in the cart. Freddie expected to capture a real sea serpent, and Dorothy declared she would bring back a whale. Nellie had an idea she would find something valuable, maybe a diamond, that some fish had swallowed in mistake for a lump of sugar at the bottom of the sea. So, with pleasant expectations, the party started off, Bert and Hal acting as guides, and leading the way.

"If you feel like climbing down the rocks here we can walk all along the edge," said Hal. "But be careful!" he cautioned, "the rocks are awfully slippery. Dorothy will have to go on ahead down the road with the donkeys, and we can meet her at the Point."

Freddie and Flossie went along with Dorothy, as the descent was considered too dangerous for the little ones. Dorothy let Freddie drive to make up for the fun the others had sliding down the rocks.

Uncle Daniel started down the cliffs first, and close behind him came Mrs. Bobbsey and Aunt Emily. Nan and Nellie took another path, if a small strip of jagged rock could be called a path, while Hal and Bert scaled down over the very roughest part, it seemed to the girls.

"Oh, mercy!" called Nan, as a rock slipped from under her foot and she promptly slipped after it. "Nellie, give me your hand or I'll slide into the ocean!"

Nellie tried to cross over to Nan, but in doing so she lost her footing and fell, then turned over twice, and only stopped as she came in contact with Uncle William's heels.

"Are you hurt?" everybody asked at once, but Nellie promptly jumped up, showing the toss had not injured her in the least.

"I thought I was going to get an unexpected bath that time," she said, laughing, "only for Mr. Minturn interfering. I saw a star in each heel of his shoe," she declared' "and I was never before glad to bump my nose."

Without further accident the party reached the sands, and saw Dorothy and the little ones a short distance away. Freddie had already filled his cap with little shells, and Flossie was busy selecting some of the finest from a collection she had made.

"Let's dig," said Hal to Bert. "There are all sorts of mussels, crabs, clams, and oysters around here. The fisheries are just above that point."

So the boys began searching in the wet sand, now and then bringing up a "fairy crab" or a baby clam.

"Here's an oyster," called Nellie, coming up with the shellfish in her hand. It was a large oyster and had been washed quite clean by the noisy waves.

"Let's open it," said Hal. "Shall I, Nellie?"

"Yes, if you want to," replied the girl, indifferently, for she did not care about the little morsel. Hal opened it easily with his knife, and then he asked who was hungry.

"Oh, see here!" he called, suddenly. "What this? It looks like a pearl."

"Let me see," said Mr. Minturn, taking the little shell in his hand, and turning out the oyster. "Yes, that surely is a pearl. Now, Nellie, you have a prize. Sometimes these little pearls are quite valuable. At any rate, you can have it set in a ring," declared Mr. Minturn.

"Oh, let me see," pleaded Dorothy. "I've always looked for pearls, and never could find one. How lucky you are, Nellie. It's worth some money."

"Maybe it isn't a pearl at all," objected Nellie, hardly believing that anything of value could be picked up so easily.

"Yes, it is," declared Mr. Minturn. "I've seen that kind before. I'll take care of it for you, and find out what it is worth," and he very carefully sealed the tiny speck in an envelope which he put in his pocketbook.

After that everybody wanted to dig for oysters, but it seemed the one that Nellie found had been washed in somehow, for the oyster beds were out in deeper water. Yet, every time Freddie found a clam or a mussel, he wanted it opened to look for pearls.

"Let us get a box of very small shells and we can string them for necklaces," suggested Nan. "We can keep them for Christmas gifts too, if we string them well."

"Oh, I've got enough for beads and bracelets," declared Flossie, for, indeed, she had lost no time in filling her box with the prettiest shells to be found on the sands.

"Oh, I see a net," called Bert, running toward a lot of driftwood in which an old net was tangled. Bert soon disentangled it and it proved to be a large piece of seine, the kind that is often used to decorate walls in libraries.

"Just what I wanted!" he declared. "And smell the salt. I will always have the ocean in my room now, for I can close my eyes and smell the salt water."

"It is a good piece," declared Hal. "You were lucky to find it. Those sell for a couple of dollars to art dealers."

"Well, I won't sell mine at any price," Bert said. "I've been wishing for a net to put back of my swords and Indian arrows. They make a fine decoration."

The grown folks had come up now, and all agreed the seine was a very pretty one.

"Well, I declare!" said Uncle William, "I have often looked for a piece of net and never could get that kind. You and Nellie were the lucky ones to-day."

"Oh, oh, oh!" screamed Freddie. "What's that?" and before he had a chance to think, he ran down to the edge of the water to meet a big barrel that had been washed in.

"Look out!" screamed Bert, but Freddie was looking in, and at that moment the water washed in right over Freddie's shoes, stockings, and all.

"Oh!" screamed everybody in chorus, for the next instant a stronger wave came in and knocked Freddie down. Quick as a flash Dorothy, who was nearest the edge, jumped in after Freddie, for as the wave receded the little boy fell in again, and might have been washed out into real danger if he had not been promptly rescued.

But as it was he was dripping wet, even his curls had been washed, and his linen suit looked just like one of Dinah's dish towels. Dorothy, too, was wet to the knees, but she did not mind that. The day was warming up and she could get along without shoes or stockings until she reached home.

"Freddie's always fallin' in," gasped Flossie, who was always getting frightened at her twin brother's accidents.

"Well, I get out, don't I?" pouted Freddie, not feeling very happy in his wet clothing.

"Now we must hurry home," insisted Mrs. Bobbsey, as she put Freddie in the donkey cart, while Dorothy, after pulling off her wet shoes and stockings, put a robe over her feet, whipped up the donkeys, Doodle and Dandy, and with Freddie and Flossie in the seat of the cart, the shells and net in the bottom, started off towards the cliffs, there to fix Freddie up in dry clothing. Of course he was not "wet to the skin," as he said, but his shoes and stockings were soaked, and his waist was wet, and that was enough. Five minutes later Dorothy pulled up the donkeys at the kitchen door, where Dinah took Freddie in her arms, and soon after fixed him up.

"You is de greatest boy for fallin' in," she declared. "Nebber saw sech a faller. But all de same you'se Dinah's baby boy," and kind-hearted Dinah rubbed Freddie's feet well, so he would not take cold; then, with fresh clothing, she made him just as comfortable and happy as he had been when he had started out shell hunting.

Downy on the Ocean

"Harry is coming to-day," Bert told Freddie, on the morning following the shell hunt, "and maybe Aunt Sarah will come with him. I'm going to get the cart now to drive over to the station. You may come along, Freddie, mother said so. Get your cap and hurry up," and Bert rushed off to the donkey barn to put Doodle and Dandy in harness.

Freddie was with Bert as quickly as he could grab his cap off the rack, and the two brothers promptly started for the station.

"I hope they bring peaches," Freddie said, thinking of the beautiful peaches in the Meadow Brook orchard that had not been quite ripe when the Bobbseys left the country for the seaside.

Numbers of people were crowded around the station when the boys got there, as the summer season was fast waning, so that Bert and Freddie had hard work to get a place near the platform for their cart.

"That's the train!" cried Bert. "Now watch out so that we don't miss them in the crowd," and the older brother jumped out of the cart to watch the faces as they passed along.

"There he is," cried Freddie, clapping his hands. "Harry! Harry! Aunt Sarah!" he called, until everybody around the station was looking at him.

"Here we are!" exclaimed Aunt Sarah the next minute, having heard Freddie's voice, and followed it to the cart.

"I'm so glad you came," declared Bert to Harry.

"And I'm awfully glad you came," Freddie told Aunt Sarah, when she stopped kissing him.

"But we cannot ride in that little cart," Aunt Sarah said, as Bert offered to help her in.

"Oh, yes, you can," Bert assured her. "These donkeys are very strong, and so is the cart. Put your satchel right in here," and he shoved the valise up in front, under the seat.

"But we have a basket of peaches somewhere," said Aunt Sarah. "They came in the baggage car."

"Oh goody! goody!" cried Freddie, clapping his little brown hands. "Let's get them."

"No, we had better have them sent over," Bert insisted, knowing that the basket would take up too much room, also that Freddie might want to sample the peaches first, and so make trouble in the small cart. Much against his will the little fellow left the peaches, and started off for the cliffs.

The girls, Dorothy, Nellie, and Nan, were waiting at the driveway, and all shouted a welcome to the people from Meadow Brook.

"You just came in time," declared Dorothy. "We are going to have a boat carnival tomorrow, and they expect it will be lovely this year."

Aunt Emily and Mrs. Bobbsey met the others now, and extended such a hearty welcome, there could be no mistaking how pleased they all were to see Harry and Aunt Sarah. As soon as Harry had a chance to lay his traveling things aside Bert and Freddie began showing him around.

"Come on down to the lake, first," Bert insisted. "Hal Bingham may have his canoe out. He's a fine fellow, and we have splendid times together."

"And you'll see my duck, Downy," said Freddie. "Oh, he's growed so big—he's just like a turkey."

Harry thought Downy must be a queer duck if he looked that way, but, of course, he did not question Freddie's description.

"Here, Downy, Downy!" called Freddie, as they came to the little stream where the duck always swam around. But there was no duck to be seen.

"Where is he?" Freddie asked, anxiously.

"Maybe back of some stones," ventured Harry. Then he and Bert joined in the search, but no duck was to be found.

"That's strange," Bert reflected. "He's always around here."

"Where does the lake run to?" Harry inquired.

"Into the ocean," answered Bert; "but Downy never goes far. There's Hal now. We'll get in his boat and see if we can find the duck."

Hal, seeing his friends, rowed in to the shore with his father's new rowboat that he was just trying.

"We have lost Freddie's duck," said Bert. "Have you seen him anywhere?"

"No, I just came out," replied Hal. "But get in and we'll go look for him."

"This is my Cousin Harry I told you about," said Bert, introducing Harry, and the two boys greeted each other, cordially.

All four got into the boat, and Harry took care of Freddie while the other boys rowed.

"Oh. I'm afraid someone has stoled Downy," cried Freddie, "and maybe they'll make—make—pudding out of him."

"No danger," said Hal, laughing. "No one around here would touch your duck. But he might have gotten curious to see the ocean. He certainly doesn't seem to be around here."

The boys had reached the line where the little lake went in a tunnel under a road, and then opened out into the ocean.

"We'll have to leave the boat here," said Hal, "and go and ask people if Downy came down this way."

Tying up the boat to a stake, the boys crossed the bridge, and made their way through the crowd of bathers down to the waves.

"Oh, oh!" screamed Freddie. "I see him! There he is!" and sure enough, there was Downy, like a tiny speck, rolling up and down on the waves, evidently having a fine swim, and not being in the least alarmed at the mountains of water that came rolling in.

"Oh, how can we get him?" cried Freddie, nearly running into the water in his excitement.

"I don't know," Hal admitted. "He's pretty far out."

Just then a life-saver came along. Freddie always insisted the life-guards were not white people, because they were so awfully browned from the sun, and really, this one looked like some foreigner, for he was almost black.

"What's the trouble?" he asked, seeing Freddie's distress.

"Oh, Downy is gone!" cried the little fellow in tears now.

"Gone!" exclaimed the guard, thinking Downy was some boy who had swam out too far.

"Yes, see him out there," sobbed Freddie, and before the other boys had a chance to tell the guard that Downy was only a duck, the life-saver was in his boat, and pulling out toward the spot where Freddie said Downy was "downing"!

"There's someone drowning!" went up the cry all around. Then numbers of men and boys, who had been bathing, plunged into the waves, and followed the life-saver out to the deeper water.

It was useless for Harry, Hal, or Bert to try to explain to anyone about the duck, for the action of the life-saver told a different story. Another guard had come down to the beach now, and was getting his ropes ready, besides opening up the emergency case, that was locked in the boat on the shore.

"Wait till they find out," whispered Hal to Bert, watching the guard in the boat nearing the white speck on the waves. It was a long ways out, but the boys could see the guard stop rowing.

"He's got him," shouted the crowd, also seeing the guard pick something out of the water. "I guess he had to lay him in the bottom of the boat."

"Maybe he's dead!" the people said, still believing the life-saver had been after some unfortunate swimmer.

"Oh, he's got him! He's got him!" cried Freddie, joyfully, still keeping up the mistake for the sightseers.

As the guard in the boat had his back to shore, and pulled in that way, even his companion on land had not yet discovered his mistake, and he waited to help revive whoever lay in the bottom of the boat.

The crowd pressed around so closely now that Freddie's toes were painfully trampled upon.

"He's mine," cried the little fellow. "Let me have him."

"It's his brother," whispered a sympathetic boy, almost in tears. "Let him get over by the boat," and so the crowd made room for Freddie, as the life-saver pulled up on the beach.

The people held their breath.

"He's dead!" insisted a number, when there was no move in the bottom of the boat. Then the guard stooped down and brought up—Downy!

"Only a duck!" screamed all the boys in the crowd, while the other life-saver laughed heartily over his preparations to restore a duck to consciousness.

"He's mine! He's mine!" insisted Freddie, as the life-saver fondled the pretty white duck, and the crowd cheered.

"Yes, he does belong to my little brother," Bert said, "and he didn't mean to fool you at all. It was just a mistake," the older brother apologized.

"Oh, I know that," laughed the guard. "But when we think there is any danger we don't wait for particulars. He's a very pretty duck all the same, and a fine swimmer, and I'm glad I got him for the little fellow, for likely he would have kept on straight out to smooth water. Then he would never have tried to get back."

The guard now handed Downy over to his young owner, and without further remarks than "Thank you," Freddie started off through the crowd, while everybody wanted to see the wonderful duck. The joke caused no end of fun, and it took Harry, Hal, and Bert to save Freddie and Downy from being too roughly treated, by the boys who were over-curious to see both the wonderful duck and the happy owner.

Real Indians

"Now we will have to watch Downy or he will be sure to take that trip again," said Bert, as they reached home with the enterprising duck.

"We could build a kind of dam across the narrowest part of the lake," suggested Hal; "kind of a close fence he would not go through. See, over there it is only a little stream, about five feet wide. We can easily fence that up. I've got lots of material up in our garden house."

"That would be a good idea," agreed Bert. "We can put Downy in the barn until we get it built. We won't take any more chances." So Downy was shut up in his box, back of the donkey stall, for the rest of the day.

"How far back do these woods run?" Harry asked his companions, he always being interested in acres, as all real country boys are.

"I don't know," Hal Bingham answered. "I never felt like going to the end to find out. But they say the Indians had reservations out here not many years ago."

"Then I'll bet there are lots of arrow heads and stone hatchets around. Let's go look. Have we time before dinner, Bert?" Harry asked.

"I guess so," replied the cousin. "Uncle William's train does not get in until seven, and we can be back by that time. We'll have to slip away from Freddie, though. Here he comes. Hide!" and at this the boys got behind things near the donkey house, and Freddie, after calling and looking around, went back to the house without finding the "boy boys."

"We can cross the lake in my boat," said Hal, as they left their hiding-places. "Then, we will be right in the woods. I'll tie the boat on the other side until we come back; no one will touch it."

"Is there no bridge?" Harry asked.

"Not nearer than the crossings, away down near the ocean beach," said Bert. "But the boat will be all right. There are no thieves around here."

It was but a few minutes' work to paddle across the lake and tie up the canoe on the opposite shore. Hal and Bert started off, feeling they would find something interesting, under Harry's leadership.

It was quite late in the afternoon, and the thick pines and ferns made the day almost like night, as the boys tramped along.

"Fine big birds around here," remarked Harry, as the feathered creatures of the ocean darted through the trees, making their way to the lake's edge.

"Yes, we're planning for a Thanksgiving shoot," Hal told him. "We hope, if we make it up, you can come down."

"I'd like to first-rate," said Harry. "Hello!" he suddenly exclaimed, "I thought I kicked over a stone hatchet head."

Instantly the three boys were on their knees searching through the brown pine needles.

"There it is!" declared Harry, picking up a queer-shaped stone. "That's real Indian—I know. Father has some, but this is the first I was ever lucky enough to find."

The boys examined the stone. There were queer marks on it, but they were so worn down it was impossible to tell what they might mean.

"What tribe camped here?" asked Harry.

"I don't know," answered Hal. "I just heard an old farmer, out Berkley way, talking about the Indians. You see, we only come down here in the summer time. Then we keep so close to the ocean we don't do much exploring "

The boys were so interested now they did not notice how dark it was getting. Neither did they notice the turns they were making in the deep woodlands. Now and then a new stone would attract their attention. They would kick it over, pick it up, and if it were of queer shape it would be pocketed for further inspection.

"Say," said Hal, suddenly, "doesn't it look like night?" and at that he ran to a clear spot between the trees, where he might see the sky.

"Sure as you live it is night!" he called back to the others. "We better pick the trail back to our canoe, or we may have to become real Indians and camp out here in spite of our appetites."

Then the boys discovered that the trees were much alike, and there were absolutely no paths to follow.

"Well, there's where the sun went down, so we must turn our back to that," advised Hal, as they tramped about, without making any progress toward finding the way home.

What at first seemed to be fun, soon turned out to be a serious matter; for the boys really could not find their way home. Each, in turn, thought he had the right way, but soon found he was mistaken.

"Well, I'll give up!" said Hal. "To think we could be lost like three babies!"

"Only worse," added Harry, "for little fellows would cry and someone might help them."

"Oh! oh! oh! oh! we're lost! We're the babes in the woods!" shouted Bert at the top of his voice, joking, yet a little in earnest.

"Let's build a fire," suggested Harry. "That's the way the Indians used to do. When our comrades see the smoke of the fire they will come and rescue us."

The other boys agreed to follow the chief's direction. So they set to work. It took some time to get wood together, and to start the fire, but when it was finally lighted, they sat around it and wasted a lot of time. It would have been better had they tried to get out of the woods, for as they waited, it grew darker.

"I wouldn't mind staying here all night," drawled Harry, stretching himself out on the dry leaves alongside the fire.

"Well, I'd like supper first," put in Hal. "We were to have roast duck to-night," and he smacked his lips.

"What was that!" Harry exclaimed, jumping up.

"A bell, I thought," whispered Hal, quite frightened.

"Indians!" added Bert. "Oh, take me home!" he wailed, and while he tried to laugh, it was a failure, for he really felt more like crying.

"There it is again. A cow bell!" declared Harry, who could not be mistaken on bells.

"Let's find the cow and maybe she will then find us," he suggested, starting off in the direction that the "tink-tink-tink-tink" came from.

"Here she is!" he called, the next moment, as he walked up to a pretty little cow with the bell on her neck. "Now, where do you belong?" Harry asked the cow. "Do you know where the Cliffs are, and how we can get home?"

The cow was evidently hungry for her supper, and bellowed loud and long. Then she rubbed her head against Harry's sleeve, and started to walk through the dark woods.

"If we follow her she will take us out, all right," said Harry, and so the three boys willingly started off after the cow.

Just as Harry had said, she made her way to a path, then the rest of the way was clear.

"Hurrah!" shouted Hal, "I smell supper already," and now, at the end of the path, an opening in the trees showed a few scattered houses.

"Why, we are away outside of Berkley," went on Hal. "Now, we will have a long tramp home, but I'm glad even at that, for a night under the trees was not a pleasant prospect."

"We must take this cow home first," said Harry, with a farmer's instinct. "Where do you suppose she belongs?"

"We might try that house first," suggested Bert, pointing to a cottage with a small barn, a little way from the wood.

"Come, Cush," said Harry, to the strange cow, and the animal obediently walked along.

There was no need to make inquiries, for outside of the house a little woman met them.

"Oh, you've found her!" she began. "Well, my husband was just going to the pound, for that old miser of a pound master takes a cow in every chance he gets, just for the fine. Come, Daisy, you're hungry," and she patted the cow affectionately. "Now, young men, I'm obliged to you, and you have saved a poor man a day's pay, for that is just what the fine would be. If you will accept a pail of milk each, I have the cans, and would be glad to give you each a quart. You might have berries for dinner," she finished.

"We would be very glad of the milk," spoke up Harry, promptly, always wide awake and polite when there was a question that concerned farmers.

"Do you live far?" asked the woman.

"Only at the Cliffs," said Harry. "We will soon he home now. But we were lost until your cow found us. She brought us here, or we would be in the woods yet."

"Well, I do declare!" laughed the little woman, filling each of three pails from the fresh milk, that stood on a bench, under the kitchen window. "Now, our man goes right by your house to-morrow morning, and if you leave the pails outside he will get them. Maybe your mothers might like some fresh milk, or buttermilk, or fresh eggs, or new butter?" she asked.

"Shouldn't wonder," said Hal. "We have hard work to get fresh stuff; they seem to send it all to the hotels. I'll let the man know when he comes for the pails."

"Thank you, thank you," replied the little woman, "and much obliged for bringing Daisy home. If you ever want a drink of milk, and are out this way, just knock at my door and I'll see you don't go away thirsty."

After more thanks on both sides, the lost boys started homeward, like a milk brigade, each with his bright tin pail of sweet new milk in his hand.

The Boat Carnival

"It didn't seem right to take all this milk," remarked Hal, as the three boys made their way in the dark, along the ocean road.

"But we would have offended the lady had we refused," said Harry. "Besides, we may be able to get her good customers by giving out the samples," he went on. "I'm sure it is good milk, for the place was clean, and that cow we found, or that found us, was a real Jersey."

The other boys did not attempt to question Harry's right to give expert views where cows and milk were concerned; so they made their way along without further comment.

"I suppose our folks will think we are lost," ventured Hal.

"Then they will think right," admitted Bert, "for that was just what we were, lost."

Crossing the bridge, the boys could hear voices.

"That's father," declared Hal. Then they listened.

"And that's Uncle William," said Bert, as another voice reached them.

"Gracious! I'm sorry this happened the first day I came," spoke up Harry, realizing that the other boys would not have gone into the deep woods if he had not acted as leader.

"Here we are!" called Hal.

"Hello there! That you, Hal?" came a call.

"Yes; we're coming," Hal answered, and the lost boys quickened their steps, as much as the pails of milk allowed.

Presently Uncle William and Mr. Bingham came up, and were so glad to find that Hal, Harry, and Bert were safe, they scarcely required any explanation for the delay in getting home. Of course, both men had been boys themselves, and well remembered how easy it was to get lost, and be late reaching home.

The milk pails, too, bore out the boys' story, had there been any doubt about it, but beyond a word of caution about dangerous places in deep woodlands there was not a harsh word spoken.

A little farther on the road home, Dorothy, Nan, and Nellie met the wanderers, and then the woodland escapade seemed a wild tale about bears, Indians, and even witches, for each girl added, to the boys' story, so much of her own imagination that the dark night and the roaring of the ocean, finished up a very wild picture, indeed.

"Now, you are real heroes," answered Dorothy, "and you are the bravest boys I know. I wish I had been along. Just think of sitting by a campfire in a dark woods, and having no one to bring you home but a poor little cow!" and Dorothy insisted on carrying Bert's milk pail to show her respect for a real hero.

Even Dinah and Susan did not complain about serving a late dinner to the boys, and both maids said they had never before seen such perfectly splendid milk as came from the farmhouse.

"We really might take some extra milk from that farm," said Aunt Emily, "for what we get is nothing like as rich in cream as this is."

So, as Harry said, the sample brought good results, for on the following morning, when the man called for the empty pail, Susan ordered two quarts a day, besides some fresh eggs and new butter to be delivered twice a week.

"Do you know," said Uncle William to Mrs. Bobbsey next morning at breakfast, when the children had left the table, "Mr. Bingham was telling me last night that his brother is at sea, on just such a voyage as little Nellie's father went on. And a man named McLaughlin went with him, too. Now, that's Nellie's name, and I believe George Bingham is the very man he went with."

"You don't tell me!" exclaimed Mrs. Bobbsey. "And have they heard any news from Mr. Bingham's brother?"

"Nothing very definite, but a vessel sighted the schooner ten days ago. Mr. Bingham has no idea his brother is lost, as he is an experienced seaman, and the Binghams are positive it is only a matter of the schooner being disabled, and the crew having a hard time to reach port," replied Mr. Minturn.

"If Nellie's mother only knew that," said Mrs. Bobbsey.

"Tell you what I'll do," said the brother-in-law; "just give me Mrs. McLaughlin's address, and I'll go to see her to-day while I'm in town. Then I can find out whether we have the right man in mind or not."

Of course, nothing was said to Nellie about the clew to her father's whereabouts, but Mrs. Bobbsey and Aunt Emily were quite excited over it, for they were very fond of Nellie, and besides, had visited her mother and knew of the poor woman's distress.

"If it only could be true that the vessel is trying to get into port," reflected Mrs. Bobbsey. "Surely, there would be enough help along the coast to save the crew."

While this very serious matter was occupying the attention of the grown-up folks, the children were all enthusiasm over the water carnival, coming off that afternoon.

Hal and Bert were dressed like real Indians, and were to paddle in Hal's canoe, while Harry was fixed up like a student, a French explorer, and he was to row alone in Hal's father's boat, to represent Father Marquette, the discoverer of the upper Mississippi River.

It was quite simple to make Harry look like the famous discoverer, for he was tall and dark, and the robes were easily arranged with Susan's black shawl, a rough cord binding it about his waist. Uncle William's traveling cap answered perfectly for the French skullcap.

"Then I'm going to be Pocahontas," insisted Dorothy, as the boys' costumes brought her mind back to Colonial days.

"Oh, no," objected Hal, "you girls better take another period of history. We can't all be Indians."

"Well, I'll never be a Puritan, not even for fun," declared Dorothy, whose spirit of frolic was certainly quite opposite that of a Priscilla.

"Who was some famous girl or woman in American history?" asked Harry, glad to get a chance to "stick" Dorothy.

"Oh, there are lots of them," answered the girl, promptly. "Don't think that men were the only people in America who did anything worth while."

"Then be one that you particularly admire," teased Harry, knowing very well Dorothy could not, at that minute, name a single character she would care to impersonate.

"Oh, let us be real," suggested Nellie. "Everybody will be all make-believe. I saw lots of people getting ready, and I'm sure they will all look like Christmas-tree things, tinsel and paper and colored stuffs."

"What would be real?', questioned Dorothy.

"Well, the Fisherman's Daughters," Nellie said, very slowly. "We have a picture at home of two little girls waiting—for their—father."

The boys noticed Nellie's manner, and knew why she hesitated. Surely it would be real for her to be a fisherman's daughter, waiting for her father!

"Oh, good!" said Dorothy. "I've got that picture in a book, and we can copy it exactly. You and I can be in a boat alone. I can row."

"You had better have a line to my boat," suggested Harry. "It would be safer in the crowd."

It had already been decided that Flossie, Freddie, and Nan should go in the Minturn launch, that was made up to look like a Venetian gondola. Mrs. Bobbsey and Aunt Emily and Aunt Sarah were to be Italian ladies, not that they cared to be in the boat parade, but because Aunt Emily, being one of the cottagers, felt obliged to encourage the social features of the little colony.

It was quite extraordinary how quickly and how well Dorothy managed to get up her costume and Nellie's. Of course, the boys were wonderful Indians, and Harry a splendid Frenchman; Mrs. Bobbsey, Aunt Sarah, and Aunt Emily only had to add lace headpieces to their brightest dinner gowns to be like the showy Italians, while Freddie looked like a little prince in his black velvet suit, with Flossie's red sash tied from shoulder to waist, in gay court fashion. Flossie wore the pink slip that belonged under her lace dress, and on her head was a silk handkerchief pinned up at the ends, in that square quaint fashion of little ladies of Venice.

There were to be prizes, of course, for the best costumes and prettiest boats, and the judges' stand was a very showy affair, built at the bridge end of the lake.

There was plenty of excitement getting ready, but finally all hands were dressed, and the music from the lake told our friends the procession was already lining up.

Mrs. Minturn's launch was given second place, just back of the Mayor's, and Mrs. Bingham's launch, fixed up to represent an automobile, came next. Then, there were all kinds of boats, some made to represent impossible things, like big swans, eagles, and one even had a lot of colored ropes flying about it, while an automobile lamp, fixed up in a great paper head, was intended to look like a monster sea-serpent, the ropes being its fangs. By cutting out a queer face in the paper over the lighted lamp the eyes blazed, of course, while the mouth was red, and wide open, and there were horns, too, made of twisted pieces of tin, so that altogether the sea-serpent looked very fierce, indeed.

The larger boats were expected to be very fine, so that as the procession passed along the little lake the steam launches did not bring out much cheering from the crowd. But now the single boats were coming.

"Father Marquette!" cried the people, instantly recognizing the historic figure Harry represented.

So slowly his boat came along, and so solemn he looked!

Then, as he reached the judges' stand, he stood up, put his hand over his eyes, looking off in the distance, exactly like the picture of the famous French explorer.

This brought out long and loud cheering, and really Harry deserved it, for he not only looked like, but really acted, the character.

There were a few more small boats next. In one the summer girl was all lace and parasol, in another there was a rude fisherman, then; some boys were dressed to look like dandies, and they seemed to enjoy themselves more than did the people looking at them. There was also a craft fixed up to look like a small gunboat.

Hal and Bert then paddled along.

They were perfect Indians, even having their faces browned with dark powder. Susan's feather duster had been dissected to make up the boys' headgear, and two overall suits, with jumpers, had been slashed to pieces to make the Indian suits. The canoe, of course, made a great stir.

"Who are they?" everybody wanted to know. But no one could guess.

"Oh, look at this!" called the people, as an old boat with two little girls drifted along.

The Fisherman's Daughters!

Perhaps it was because there was so much gayety around that these little girls looked so real. From the side of their weather-beaten boat dragged an old fishnet. Each girl had on her head a queer half-hood, black, and from under this Nellie's brown hair fell in tangles on her bare shoulders, and Dorothy's beautiful yellow ringlets framed in her own pretty face. The children wore queer bodices, like those seen in pictures of Dutch girls, and full skirts of dark stuff finished out their costumes.

As they sat in the boat and looked out to sea, "watching for the fisherman's return," their attitude and pose were perfect.

The people did not even cheer. They seemed spellbound.

"That child is an actress," they said, noting the "real" look on Nellie's face. But Nellie was not acting. She was waiting for the lost father at sea.

When would he come back to her?

The First Prize

When the last craft in the procession had passed the judges' stand, and the little lake was alive with decorations and nautical novelties, everybody, of course, in the boats and on land, was anxious to know who would get the prizes.

There were four to be given, and the fortunate ones could have gifts in silver articles or the value in money, just as they chose.

Everybody waited anxiously, when the man at the judges' stand stood up and called through the big megaphone:

"Let the Fisherman's Daughters pass down to the stand!"

"Oh, we are going to get a prize," Dorothy said to Nellie. "I'll just cut the line to Harry's boat and row back to the stand."

Then, when the two little girls sailed out all by themselves, Dorothy rowing gracefully, while Nellie helped some, although not accustomed to the oars, the people fairly shouted.

For a minute the girls waited in front of the stand. But the more people inspected them the better they appeared. Finally, the head judge stood up.

"First prize is awarded to the Fisherman's Daughters," he announced.

The cheering that followed his words showed the approval of the crowd. Nellie and Dorothy were almost frightened at the noise. Then they rowed their boat to the edge, and as the crowd gathered around them to offer congratulations, the other prizes were awarded.

The second prize went to the Indians!

"Lucky they don't know us," said Hal to Bert, "for they would never let the two best prizes get in one set." The Indians were certainly well made-up, and their canoe a perfect redman's bark.

The third prize went to the "Sea-serpent," for being the funniest boat in the procession; and the fourth to the gunboat. Then came a great shouting!

A perfect day had added to the success of the carnival, and now many people adjourned to the pavilion, where a reception was held, and good things to eat were bountifully served.

"But who was the little girl with Dorothy Minturn?" asked the mayor's wife. Of course everybody knew Dorothy, but Nellie was a stranger.

Mrs. Minturn, Mrs. Bobbsey, Aunt Sarah, Mrs. Bingham, and Mrs. Blake, the latter being the mayor's wife, had a little corner in the pavilion to themselves. Here Nellie's story was quietly told.

"How nice it was she got the prize," said Mrs. Blake, after hearing about Nellie's hardships. "I think we had better have it in money—and we might add something to it," she suggested. "I am sure Mr. Blake would be glad to. He often gives a prize himself. I'll just speak to him."

Of course Dorothy was to share the prize, and she accepted a pretty silver loving cup. But what do you suppose they gave Nellie?

Fifty dollars!

Was not that perfectly splendid?

The prize for Nellie was twenty-five dollars, but urged by Mrs. Blake, the mayor added to it his own check for the balance.

Naturally Nellie wanted to go right home to her mother with it, and nothing about the reception had any interest for her after she received the big check. However, Mrs. Bobbsey insisted that Mr. Minturn would take the money to Nellie's mother the next day, so the little girl had to be content.

Then, when all the festivities were over, and the children's excitement had brought them to bed very tired that night, Nellie sat by her window and looked out at the sea!

Always the same prayer, but to-night, somehow, it seemed answered!

Was it the money for mother that made the father seem so near?

The roaring waves seemed to call out:

"Nellie—Nellie dear! I'm coming—coming home to you!"

And while the little girl was thus dreaming upstairs, Mr. Minturn down in the library was telling about his visit to Nellie's mother.

"There is no doubt about it," he told Mrs. Bobbsey. "It was Nellie's father who went away with George Bingham, and it was certainly that schooner that was sighted some days ago."

The ladies, of course, were overjoyed at the prospect of the best of luck for Nellie—her father's possible return,—and then it was decided that Uncle William should again go to Mrs. McLaughlin, this time to take her the prize money, and that Mrs. Bobbsey should go along with him, as it was such an important errand.

"And you remember that little pearl that Nellie found on the beach? Well, I'm having it set in a ring for her. It is a real pearl, but not very valuable, yet I thought it would be a souvenir of her visit at the Cliffs," said Mr. Minturn.

"That will be very nice," declared Mrs. Bobbsey. "I am sure no one deserves to be made happy more than that child does, for just fancy, how she worked in that store as cash girl until her health gave way. And now she is anxious to go back to the store again. Of course she is worried about her mother, but the prize money ought to help Mrs. McLaughlin so that Nellie would not need to cut her vacation short."

"What kind of treasure was it that these men went to sea after?" Aunt Emily asked Uncle William.

"A cargo of mahogany," Mr. Minturn replied. "You see, that wood is scarce now, a cargo is worth a fortune, and a shipload was being brought from the West Indies to New York when a storm blew the vessel out to a very dangerous point. Of course, the vessel was wrecked, and so were two others that later attempted to reach the valuable cargo. You see the wind always blows the one way there, and it is impossible to get the mahogany out of its trap. Now, George Bingham was offered fifty thousand dollars to bring that wood to port, and he decided that he could do it by towing each log around the reef by canoes. The logs are very heavy, each one is worth between eighty and one hundred dollars, but the risk meant such a reward, in case of success, that they went at it. Of course the real danger is around the wreck. Once free from that point and the remainder of the voyage would be only subject to the usual ocean storms."

"And those men were to go through the dangerous waters in little canoes!" exclaimed Aunt Emily.

"But the danger was mostly from winds to the sails of vessels," explained Uncle William. "Small craft are safest in such waters."

"And if they succeeded in bringing the mahogany in?" asked Mrs. Bobbsey.

"Nellie would be comparatively rich, for her father went as George Bingham's partner," finished Mr. Minturn.

So, the evening went into night, and Nellie, the Fisherman's Daughter, slept on, to dream that the song of the waves came true.

Lost on an Island

The calm that always follows a storm settled down upon the Cliffs the day after the carnival. The talk of the entire summer settlement was Nellie and her prize, and naturally, the little girl herself thought of home and the lonely mother, who was going to receive such a surprise—fifty dollars!

It was a pleasant morning, and Freddie and Flossie were out watching Downy trying to get through the fence that the boys had built to keep him out of the ocean. Freddie had a pretty little boat Uncle William had brought down from the city. It had sails, that really caught the wind, and carried the boat along.

Of course Freddie had a long cord tied to it, so it could not get out of his reach, and while Flossie tried to steer the vessel with a long whip, Freddie made believe he was a canal man, and walked along the tow path with the cord in hand.

"I think I would have got a prize in the boat parade if I had this steamer," said Freddie, feeling his craft was really as fine as any that had taken part in the carnival.

"Maybe you would," agreed Flossie. "Now let me sail it a little."

"All right," said Freddie, and he offered the cord to his twin sister.

"Oh," she exclaimed, "I dropped it!"

The next minute the little boat made a turn with the breeze, and before Flossie could get hold of the string it was all in the water!

"Oh, my boat!" cried Freddie. "Get it quick!"

"I can't!" declared Flossie. "It is out too far! Oh, what shall we do!"

"Now you just get it! You let it go," went on the brother, without realizing that his sister could not reach the boat, nor the string either, for that matter.

"Oh, it's going far away!" cried Flossie; almost in tears.

The little boat was certainly making its way out into the lake, and it sailed along so proudly, it must have been very glad to be free.

"There's Hal Bingham's boat," ventured Flossie. "Maybe I could go out a little ways in that."

"Of course you can," promptly answered Freddie. "I can row."

"I don't know, we might upset!" Flossie said, hesitating.

"But it isn't deep. Why, Downy walks around out here," went on the brother.

This assurance gave the little girl courage, and slipping the rope off the peg that secured the boat to the shore, very carefully she put Freddie on one seat, while she sat herself on the other.

The oars were so big she did not attempt to handle them, but just depended on the boat to do its own sailing.

"Isn't this lovely!" declared Freddie, as the boat drifted quietly along.

"Yes, but how can we get back?" asked Flossie, beginning to realize their predicament.

"Oh, easy!" replied Freddie, who suddenly seemed to have become a man, he was so brave. "The tide comes down pretty soon, and then our boat will go back to shore."

Freddie had heard so much about the tide he felt he understood it perfectly. Of course, there was no tide on the lake, although the waters ran lazily toward the ocean at times.

"But we are not getting near my boat," Freddie complained, for indeed the toy sailboat was drifting just opposite their way.

"Well, I can't help it, I'm sure," cried Flossie. "And I just wish I could get back. I'm going to call somebody."

"Nobody can hear you," said her brother. "They are all down by the ocean, and there's so much noise there you can't even hear thunder."

Where the deep woods joined the lake there was a little island. This was just around the turn, and entirely out of view of either the Minturn or the Bingham boat landing. Toward this little island the children's boat was now drifting.

"Oh, we'll be real Robinson Crusoes!" exclaimed Freddie, delighted at the prospect of such an adventure.

"I don't want to be no Robinson Crusoe!" pouted his sister. "I just want to get back home," and she began to cry.

"We're going to bunk," announced Freddie, as at that minute the boat did really bump into the little island. "Come, Flossie, let us get ashore," said the brother, in that superior way that had come to him in their distress.

Flossie willingly obeyed.

"Be careful!" she cautioned. "Don't step out till I get hold of your hand. It is awfully easy to slip getting out of a boat."

Fortunately for the little ones they had been taught to be careful when around boats, so that they were able to take care of themselves pretty well, even in their present danger.

Once on land, Flossie's fears left her, and she immediately set about picking the pretty little water flowers, that grew plentifully among the ferns and flag lilies.

"I'm going to build a hut," said Freddie, putting pieces of dry sticks up against a willow tree. Soon the children became so interested they did not notice their boat drift away, and really leave them all alone on the island!

In the meantime everybody at the house was looking for the twins. Their first fear, of course, was the ocean, and down to the beach Mrs. Bobbsey, Aunt Sarah, and the boys hurried, while Aunt Emily and the girls made their way to the Gypsy Camp, fearing the fortune tellers might have stolen the children in order to get money for bringing them back again.

Dorothy walked boldly up to the tent. An old woman sat outside and looked very wicked, her face was so dark and her hair so black and tangled.

"Have you seen a little boy and girl around here?" asked Dorothy, looking straight into the tent.

"No, nobody round here. Tell your fortune, lady?" This to Aunt Emily, who waited for Dorothy.

"Not to-day," answered Aunt Emily. "We are looking for two children. Are you sure you have not seen them?"

"No, lady. Gypsy tell lady's fortune, then lady find them," she suggested, with that trick her class always uses, trying to impose on persons in trouble with the suggestion of helping them out of it.

"No, we have not time," insisted Aunt Emily; really quite alarmed now that there was no trace of the little twins.

"Let me look through your tent?" asked Dorothy, bravely.

"What for?" demanded the old woman.

"To make sure the children are not hiding," and without waiting for a word from the old woman, Dorothy walked straight into that gypsy tent!

Even Aunt Emily was frightened.

Suppose somebody inside should keep Dorothy?

"Come out of my house!" muttered the woman, starting after Dorothy.

"Come out, Dorothy," called her mother, but the girl was making her way through the old beds and things inside, to make sure there was no Freddie or Flossie to be found in the tent.

It was a small place, of course, and it did not take Dorothy very long to search it.

Presently she appeared again, much to the relief of her mother, Nan, and Nellie, who waited breathlessly outside.

"They are not around here," said Dorothy. "Now, mother, give the old woman some change to make up for my trespassing."

Aunt Emily took a coin from her chatelaine.

"Thank the lady! Good lady," exclaimed the old gypsy. "Lady find her babies; babies play—see!" (And she pretended to look into the future with some dirty cards.) "Babies play in woods. Natalie sees babies picking flowers."

Now, how could anybody ever guess that the old gypsy had just come down from picking dandelions by the lake, where she really had seen Freddie and Flossie on the island?

And how could anybody know that she was too wicked to tell Aunt Emily this, but was waiting until night, to bring the children back home herself, and get a reward for doing so?

She had seen the boat drift away and she knew the little ones were helpless to return home unless someone found them.

Mrs. Bobbsey and the boys were now coming up from the beach.

What, at first, seemed only a mishap, now looked like a very serious matter.

"We must go to the woods," insisted Dorothy. "Maybe that old woman knew they were in the woods."

But as such things always happen, the searchers went to the end of the woods, far away from the island. Of course they all called loudly, and the boys gave the familiar yodel, but the noise of the ocean made it impossible for the call to reach Freddie and Flossie.

"Oh, I'm so afraid they are drowned!" exclaimed Mrs. Bobbsey, breaking down and crying.

"No, mamma," insisted Nan, "I am sure they are not. Flossie is so afraid of the water, and Freddie always minds Flossie. They must be playing somewhere. Maybe they are home by this time," and so it was agreed to go back to the house and if the little ones were not there—then—-

"But they must be there," insisted Nellie, starting on a run over the swampy grounds toward the Cliffs.

And all this time Freddie and Flossie were quite unconcerned playing on the island.

"Oh, there's a man!" shouted Freddie, seeing someone in the woods. "Maybe it's Friday. Say there, Mister!" he shouted. "Say, will you help us get to land?"

The man heard the child's voice and hurried to the edge of the lake.

"Wall, I declare!" he exclaimed, "if them babies ain't lost out there. And here comes their boat. Well, I'll just fetch them in before they try to swim out," he told himself, swinging into the drifting boat, and with the stout stick he had in his hand, pushing off for the little island.

The island was quite near to shore on that side, and it was only a few minutes' work for the man to reach the children.

"What's your name?" he demanded, as soon as he touched land.

"Freddie Bobbsey," spoke up the little fellow, bravely, "and we live at the Cliffs."

"You do, eh? Then it was your brothers who brought my cow home, so I can pay them back by taking you home now. I can't row to the far shore with this stick, so we'll have to tramp it through the woods. Come along." and carefully he lifted the little ones into the boat, pushing to the woods, and started off to walk the round-about way, through the woods, to the bridge, then along the road back to the Cliffs, where a whole household was in great distress because of the twins' absence.

Dorothy's Doings

"Here they come!" called Nellie, who was searching around the barn, and saw the farmer with the two children crossing the hill.

"I'm Robinson Crusoe!" insisted Freddie, "and this is my man, Friday," he added, pointing to the farmer.

Of course it did not take long to clear up the mystery of the little ones' disappearance. But since his return Freddie acted like a hero, and certainly felt like one, and Flossie brought home with her a dainty bouquet of pink sebatia, that rare little flower so like a tiny wild rose. The farmer refused to take anything for his time and trouble, being glad to do our friends a favor.

Aunt Sarah and Harry were to leave for Meadow Brook that afternoon, but the worry over the children being lost made Aunt Sarah feel quite unequal to the journey, so Aunt Emily prevailed upon her to wait another day.

"There are so many dangers around here," remarked Aunt Sarah, when all the "scare" was over. "It is different in the country. We never worry about lost children out in Meadow Brook."

"But I often got lost out there," insisted Freddie. "Don't you remember?"

Aunt Sarah had some recollection of the little fellow's adventures in that line, and laughed over them, now that they were recalled.

Late that afternoon Dorothy, Nan, and Nellie had a conference: that is, they talked with their heads so close together not even Flossie could get an idea of what they were planning. But it was certainly mischief, for Dorothy had most to say, and she would rather have a good joke than a good dinner any day, so Susan said.

Harry, Hal, and Bert had been chasing through the woods after a queer-looking bird. It was large, and had brilliant feathers, and when it rested for a moment on a tree it would pick at the bark as if it were trying to play a tune with its beak. Each time it struck the bark its head bobbed up and down in a queer way for a bird. But the boys could not get it. They set Hal's trap, and even used an air rifle in hopes of bringing it down without killing it, but the bird puttered from place to place, not in a very great hurry, but just fast enough to keep the boys busy chasing it.

That evening, at dinner, the strange bird was much talked about.

"Dat's a ban-shee!" declared Dinah, jokingly. "Dat bird came to bring a message from somebody. You boys will hear dat tonight, see if you doesn't," and she gave a very mysterious wink at Dorothy, who just then nearly choked with her dessert.

A few hours later the house was all quiet. The happenings of the day brought a welcome night, and tired little heads comfortably hugged their pillows.

It must have been about midnight, Bert was positive he had just heard the clock strike a lot of rings, surely a dozen or so, when at his window came a queer sound, like something pecking. At first Bert got it mixed up with his dreams, but as it continued longer and louder, he called to Harry, who slept in the alcove in Bert's room, and together the boys listened, attentively.

"That's the strange bird," declared Harry. "Sure enough it is bringing us a message, as Dinah said," and while the boys took the girl's words in a joke, they really seemed to be coming true.

"Don't light the gas," cautioned Bert, "or that will surely frighten it off. We can get our air guns, and I'll go crawl out on the veranda roof back of it, so as to get it if possible."

All this time the "peck-peck-peck" kept at the window, but just as soon as Bert went out in the hall to make his way through the storeroom window to the veranda roof, the pecking ceased. Harry hurried after Bert to tell him the bird was gone, and then together the boys put their heads out of their own window.

But there was not a sound, not even the distant flutter of a bird's wing to tell the boys the messenger had gone.

"Back to bed for us," said Harry, laughing. "I guess that bird is a joker and wants to keep us busy," and both boys being healthy were quite ready to fall off to sleep as soon as they felt it was of no use to stay awake longer looking for their feathered visitor.

"There it is again," called Bert, when Harry had just begun to dream of hazelnuts in Meadow Brook. "I'll get him this time!" and without waiting to go through the storeroom, Bert raised the window and bolted out on the roof.

"What's de matter down dere?" called Dinah from the window above. "'Pears like as if you boys had de nightmare. Can't you let nobody get a wink ob sleep? Ebbery time I puts my head down, bang! comes a noise and up pops my head. Now, what's a-ailin' ob you, Bert?" and the colored girl showed by her tone of voice she was not a bit angry, but "chock-full of laugh," as Bert whispered to Harry.

But the boys had not caught the bird, had not even seen it, for that matter.

Both Bert and Harry were now on the roof in their pajamas.

"What's—the—matter—there?" called Dorothy, in a very drowsy voice, from her window at the other end of the roof.

"What are you boys after?" called Uncle William, from a middle window.

"Anything the matter?" asked Aunt Sarah, anxiously, from the spare room.

"Got a burgulor?" shrieked Freddie, from the nursery.

"Do you want any help?" offered Susan, her head out of the top-floor window.

All these questions came so thick and fast on the heads of Bert and Harry that the boys had no idea of answering them. Certainly the bird was nowhere to be seen, and they did not feel like advertising their "April-fool game" to the whole house, so they decided to crawl into bed again and let others do the same.

The window in the boys' room was a bay, and each time the pecking disturbed them they thought the sound came from a different part of the window. Bert said it was the one at the left, so where the "bird" called from was left a mystery.

But neither boy had time to close his eyes before the noise started up again!

"Well, if that isn't a ghost it certainly is a ban-shee, as Dinah said," whispered Bert. "I'm going out to Uncle William's room and tell him. Maybe he will have better luck than we had," and so saying, Bert crept out into the hall and down two doors to his uncle's room.

Uncle William had also heard the sound.

"Don't make a particle of noise," cautioned the uncle, "and we can go up in the cupola and slide down a post so quietly the bird will not hear us," and as he said this, he, in his bath robe, went cautiously up the attic stairs, out of a small window, and slid down the post before Bert had time to draw his own breath.

But there was no bird to be seen anywhere!

"I heard it this very minute!" declared Harry, from the window.

"It might be bats!" suggested Uncle William. "But listen! I thought I heard the girls laughing," and at that moment an audible titter was making its way out of Nan's room!

"That's Dorothy's doings!" declared Uncle William, getting ready to laugh himself. "She's always playing tricks," and he began to feel about the outside ledge of the bay window.

But there was nothing there to solve the mystery.

"A tick-tack!" declared Harry, "I'll bet, from the girls' room!" and without waiting for another word he jumped out of his window, ran along the roof to Nan's room, and then grabbed something.

"Here it is!" he called, confiscating the offending property. "You just wait, girls!" he shouted in the window. "If we don't give you a good ducking in the ocean for this to-morrow!"

The laugh of the three girls in Nan's room made the joke on the boys more complete, and as Uncle William went back to his room he declared to Mrs. Bobbsey and Aunt Emily that his girl, Dorothy, was more fun than a dozen boys, and he would match her against that number for the best piece of good-natured fun ever played.

"A bird!" sneered Bert, making fun of himself for being so easily fooled.

"A girls' game of tick-tack!" laughed Harry, making up his mind that if he did not "get back at Dorothy," he would certainly have to haul in his colors as captain of the Boys' Brigade of Meadow Brook; "for she certainly did fool me," he admitted, turning over to sleep at last.

Old Friends

"Now, Aunt Sarah," pleaded Nan the next morning, "you might just as well wait and go home on the excursion train. All Meadow Brook will be down, and it will be so much pleasanter for you. The train will be here by noon and leave at three o'clock."

"But think of the hour that would bring us to Meadow Brook!" objected Aunt Sarah.

"Well, you will have lots of company, and if Uncle Daniel shouldn't meet you, you can ride up with the Hopkinses or anybody along your road."

Mrs. Bobbsey and Aunt Emily added their entreaties to Nan's, and Aunt Sarah finally agreed to wait.

"If I keep on," she said, "I'll be here all summer. And think of the fruit that's waiting to be preserved!"

"Hurrah!" shouted Bert, giving his aunt a good hug. "Then Harry and I can have a fine time with the Meadow Brook boys," and Bert dashed out to take the good news to Harry and Hal Bingham, who were out at the donkey house.

"Come on, fellows!" he called. "Down to the beach! We can have a swim before the crowd gets there." And with renewed interest the trio started off for the breakers.

"I would like to live at the beach all summer," remarked Harry. "Even in winter it must be fine here."

"It is," said Hal. "But the winds blow everything away regularly, and they all have to be carted back again each spring. This shore, with all its trimmings now, will look like a bald head by the first of December."

All three boys were fine swimmers, and they promptly struck off for the water that was "straightened out," as Bert said, beyond the tearing of the breakers at the edge. There were few people in the surf and the boys made their way around as if they owned the ocean.

Suddenly Hal thought he heard a call!

Then a man's arm appeared above the water's surface, a few yards away.

"Cramps," yelled Hal to Harry and Bert, while all three hurried to where the man's hand had been seen.

But it did not come up again.

"I'll dive down!" spluttered Hal, who had the reputation of being able to stay a long time under water.

It seemed quite a while to Bert and Harry before Hal came up again, but when he did he was trying to pull with him a big, fat man, who was all but unconscious.

"Can't move," gasped Hal, as the heavy burden was pulling him down.

Bit by bit the man with cramps gained a little strength, and with the boys' help he was towed in to shore.

There was not a life-guard in sight, and Hal had to hurry off to the pier for some restoratives, for the man was very weak. On his way, Hal met a guard who, of course, ran to the spot where Harry and Bert were giving the man artificial respiration.

"You boys did well!" declared the guard, promptly, seeing how hard they worked with the sick man.

"Yes—they saved—my life!" gasped the half-drowned man. "This little fellow"—pointing to Hal—"brought—me up—almost—from—the bottom!" and he caught his breath, painfully.

The man was assisted to a room at the end of the pier, and after a little while he became much better. Of course the boys did not stand around, being satisfied they could be of no more use.

"I must get those lads' names," declared the man to the guard. "Mine is ——," and he gave the name of the famous millionaire who had a magnificent summer home in another colony, three miles away.

"And you swam from the Cedars, Mr. Black," exclaimed the guard. "No wonder you got cramps."

An hour later the millionaire was walking the beach looking for the life-savers. He finally spied Hal.

"Here, there, you boy," he called, and Hal came in to the edge, but hardly recognized the man in street clothes.

"I want your name," demanded the stranger. "Do you know there are medals given to young heroes like you?"

"Oh, that was nothing," stammered Hal, quite confused now.

"Nothing! Why, I was about dead, and pulled on you with all my two hundred pounds. You knew, too, you had hardly a chance to bring me up. Yes, indeed, I want your name," and as he insisted, Hal reluctantly gave it, but felt quite foolish to make such a fuss "over nothing," as he said.

It was now about time for the excursion train to come in, so the boys left the water and prepared to meet their old friends.

"I hope Jack Hopkins comes," said Bert, for Jack was a great friend.

"Oh, he will be along," Harry remarked. "Nobody likes a good time better than Jack."

"Here they come!" announced Hal, the next minute, as a crowd of children with many lunch boxes came running down to the ocean.

"Hello there! Hello there!" called everybody at once, for, of course, all the children knew Harry and many also knew Bert.

There were Tom Mason, Jack Hopkins, August Stout, and Ned Prentice in the first crowd, while a number of girls, friends of Nan's, were in another group. Nan, Nellie, and Dorothy had been detained by somebody further up on the road, but were now coming down, slowly.

Such a delight as the ocean was to the country children!

As each roller slipped out on the sands the children unconsciously followed it, and so, many unsuspected pairs of shoes were caught by the next wave that washed in.

"Well, here comes Uncle Daniel!" called Bert, as, sure enough, down to the edge came Uncle Daniel with Dorothy holding on one arm, Nan clinging to the other, while Nellie carried his small satchel.

Santa Claus could hardly have been more welcome to the Bobbseys at that moment than was Uncle Daniel. They simply overpowered him, as the surprise of his coming made the treat so much better. The girls had "dragged him" down to the ocean, he said, when he had intended first going to Aunt Emily's.

"I must see the others," he insisted; "Freddie and Flossie."

"Oh, they are all coming down," Nan assured him. "Aunt Sarah, too, is coming."

"All right, then," agreed Uncle Daniel. "I'll wait awhile. Well, Harry, you look like an Indian. Can you see through that coat of tan?"

Harry laughed and said he had been an Indian in having a good time.

Presently somebody jumped up on Uncle Daniel's back. As he was sitting on the sands the shock almost brought him down. Of course it was Freddie, who was so overjoyed he really treated the good-natured uncle a little roughly.

"Freddie boy! Freddie boy!" exclaimed Uncle Daniel, giving his nephew a good long hug. "And you have turned Indian, too! Where's that sea-serpent you were going to catch for me?"

"I'll get him yet," declared the little fellow. "It hasn't rained hardly since we came down, and they only come in to land out of the rain."

This explanation made Uncle Daniel laugh heartily. The whole family sat around on the sands, and it was like being in the country and at the seashore at the one time, Flossie declared.

The boys, of course, were in the water. August Stout had not learned much about swimming since he fell off the plank while fishing in Meadow Brook, so that out in the waves the other boys had great fun with their fat friend.

"And there is Nettie Prentice!" exclaimed Nan, suddenly, as she espied her little country friend looking through the crowd, evidently searching for friends.

"Oh, Nan!" called Nettie, in delight, "I'm just as glad to see you as I am to see the ocean, and I never saw that before," and the two little girls exchanged greetings of genuine love for each other.

"Won't we have a perfectly splendid time?" declared Nan. "Dorothy, my cousin, is so jolly, and here's Nellie—you remember her?"

Of course Nettie did remember her, and now all the little girls went around hunting for fun in every possible corner where fun might be hidden.

As soon as the boys were satisfied with their bath they went in search of the big sun umbrellas, so that Uncle William, Aunt Emily, Mrs. Bobbsey, and Aunt Sarah might sit under the sunshades, while eating lunch. Then the boys got long boards and arranged them from bench to bench in picnic style, so that all the Meadow Brook friends might have a pleasant time eating their box lunches.

"Let's make lemonade," suggested Hal. "I know where I can get a pail of nice clean water."

"I'll buy the lemons," offered Harry.

"I'll look after sugar," put in Bert.

"And I'll do the mixing," declared August Stout, while all set to work to produce the wonderful picnic lemonade.

"Now, don't go putting in white sand instead of sugar," teased Uncle Daniel, as the "caterers," with sleeves rolled up, worked hard over the lemonade.

"What can we use for cups ?" asked Nan.

"Oh, I know," said Harry, "over at the Indian stand they have a lot of gourds, the kind of mock oranges that Mexicans drink out of. I can buy them for five cents each, and after the picnic we can bring them home and hang them up for souvenirs."

"Just the thing!" declared Hal, who had a great regard for things that hang up and look like curios. "I'll go along and help you make the bargain."

When the boys came back they had a dozen of the funny drinking cups.

The long crooked handles were so queer that each person tried to get the cup to his or her mouth in a different way.

"We stopped at the hydrant and washed the gourds thoroughly," declared Hal, "so you need not expect to find any Mexican diamonds in them."

"Or tarantulas," put in Uncle Daniel.

"What's them?" asked Freddie, with an ear for anything that sounded like a menagerie.

"A very bad kind of spider, that sometimes comes in fruit from other countries," explained Uncle Daniel. Then Nan filled his gourd from the dipper that stood in the big pail of lemonade, and he smacked his lips in appreciation.

There was so much to do and so much to see that the few hours allowed the excursionists slipped by all too quickly. Dorothy ran away and soon returned with her donkey cart, to take Nettie Prentice and a few of Nettie's friends for a ride along the beach. Nan and Nellie did not go, preferring to give the treat to the little country girls.

"Now don't go far," directed Aunt Emily, for Aunt Sarah and Uncle Daniel were already leaving the beach to make ready for the train. Of course Harry and Aunt Sarah were all "packed up" and had very little to do at Aunt Emily's before starting.

Hal and Bert were sorry, indeed, to have Harry go, for Harry was such a good leader in outdoor sports, his country training always standing by him in emergencies.

Finally Dorothy came back with the girls from their ride, and the people were beginning to crowd into the long line of cars that waited on a switch near the station.

"Now, Nettie, be sure to write to me," said Nan, bidding her little friend good-by.

"And come down next year," insisted Dorothy.

"I had such a lovely time," declared Nettie. "I'm sure I will come again if I can."

The Meadow Brook Bobbseys had secured good seats in the middle car,—Aunt Sarah thought that the safest,—and now the locomotive whistle was tooting, calling the few stragglers who insisted on waiting at the beach until the very last minute.

Freddie wanted to cry when he realized that Uncle Daniel, Aunt Sarah, and even Harry were going away, but with the promises of meeting again Christmas, and possibly Thanksgiving, all the good-bys were said, and the excursion train puffed out on its long trip to dear old Meadow Brook, and beyond.

The Storm

When Uncle William Minturn came in from the city that evening he had some mysterious news. Everybody guessed it was about Nellie, but as surprises were always cropping up at Ocean Cliff, the news was kept secret and the whispering increased.

"I had hard work to get her to come," said Uncle William to Mrs. Bobbsey, still guarding the mystery, "but I finally prevailed upon her and she will be down on the morning train."

"Poor woman, I am sure it will do her good," remarked Mrs. Bobbsey. "Your house has been a regular hotel this summer," she said to Mr. Minturn.

"That's what we are here for," he replied. "We would not have much pleasure, I am sure, if our friends were not around us."

"Did you hear anything more about the last vessel?" asked Aunt Emily.

"Yes, I went down to the general office today, and an incoming steamer was sure it was the West Indies vessel that was sighted four days ago."

"Then they should be near port now?" asked Mrs. Bobbsey.

"They ought to be," replied Uncle William, "but the cargo is so heavy, and the schooner such a very slow sailer, that it takes a long time to cover the distance."

Next morning, bright and early, Dorothy had the donkeys in harness.

"We are going to the station to meet some friends, Nellie," she said. "Come along?"

"What! More company?" exclaimed Nellie. "I really ought to go home. I am well and strong now."

"Indeed you can't go until we let you," said Dorothy, laughing. "I suppose you think all the fun went with Harry," she added, teasingly, for Dorothy knew Nellie had been acting lonely ever since the carnival. She was surely homesick to see her mother and talk about the big prize.

The two girls had not long to wait at the station, for the train pulled in just as they reached the platform. Dorothy looked about a little uneasily.

"We must watch for a lady in a linen suit with black hat," she said to Nellie; "she's a stranger."

That very minute the linen suit appeared.

"Oh, oh!" screamed Nellie, unable to get her words. "There is my mother!" and the next thing Dorothy knew, Nellie was trying to "wear the same linen dress" that the stranger appeared in—at least, that was how Dorothy afterwards told about Nellie's meeting with her mother.

"My daughter!" exclaimed the lady, "I have been so lonely I came to bring you home."

"And this is Dorothy," said Nellie, recovering herself. "Dorothy is my best friend, next to Nan."

"You have surely been among good friends," declared the mother, "for you have gotten the roses back in your cheeks again. How well you do look!"

"Oh, I've had a perfectly fine time," declared Nellie.

"Fine and dandy," repeated Dorothy, unable to restrain her fun-making spirit.

At a glance Dorothy saw why Nellie, although poor, was so genteel, for her mother was one of those fine-featured women that seem especially fitted to say gentle things to children.

Mrs. McLaughlin was not old,—no older than Nan's mother,—and she had that wonderful wealth of brown hair, just like Nellie's. Her eyes were brown, too, while Nellie's were blue, but otherwise Nellie was much like her mother, so people said.

Aunt Emily and Mrs. Bobbsey had visited Mrs. McLaughlin in the city, so that they were quite well acquainted when the donkey cart drove up, and they all had a laugh over the surprise to Nellie. Of course that was Uncle William's secret, and the mystery of the whispering the evening before.

"But we must go back on the afternoon train," insisted Mrs. McLaughlin, who had really only come down to the shore to bring Nellie home.

"Indeed, no," objected Aunt Emily, "that would be too much traveling in one day. You may go early in the morning."

"Everybody is going home," sighed Dorothy. "I suppose you will be the next to go, Nan," and she looked quite lonely at the prospect.

"We are going to have a big storm," declared Susan, who had just come in from the village. "We have had a long dry spell, now we are going to make up for it."

"Dear me," sighed Mrs. McLaughlin, "I wish we had started for home."

"Oh, there's lots of fun here in a storm," laughed Dorothy. "The ocean always tries to lick up the whole place, but it has to be satisfied with pulling down pavilions and piers. Last year the water really went higher than the gas lights along the boulevard."

"Then that must mean an awful storm at sea," reflected Nellie's mother. "Storms are bad enough on land, but at sea they must be dreadful!" And she looked out toward the wild ocean, that was keeping from her the fate of her husband.

Long before there were close signs of storm, life-guards, on the beach, were preparing for it. They were making fast everything that could be secured and at the life-saving station all possible preparations were being made to help those who might suffer from the storm.

It was nearing September and a tidal wave had swept over the southern ports. Coming in all the way from the tropics the storm had made itself felt over a great part of the world, in some places taking the shape of a hurricane.

On this particular afternoon, while the sun still shone brightly over Sunset Beach, the storm was creeping in under the big waves that dashed up on the sands.

"It is not safe to let go the ropes," the guards told the people, but the idea of a storm, from such a pretty sky, made some daring enough to disobey these orders. The result was that the guards were kept busy trying to bring girls and women to their feet, who were being dashed around by the excited waves.

This work occupied the entire afternoon, and as soon as the crowd left the beach the life-guards brought the boats down to the edge, got their lines ready, and when dark came on, they were prepared for the life-patrol,—the long dreary watch of the night, so near the noisy waves, and so far from the voice of distress that might call over the breakers to the safe shores, where the life-savers waited, watched, and listened.

The rain began to fall before it was entirely dark. The lurid sunset, glaring through the dark and rain, gave an awful, yellow look to the land and sea alike.

"It is like the end of the world," whispered Nellie to Nan, as the two girls looked out of the window to see the wild storm approaching.

Then the lightning came in blazing blades, cutting through the gathering clouds.

The thunder was only like muffled rolls, for the fury of the ocean deadened every other sound of heaven or earth.

"It will be a dreadful storm," said Aunt Emily to Mrs. Bobbsey. "We must all go into the sitting room and pray for the sailors."

Everyone in the house assembled in the large sitting room, and Uncle William led the prayers. Poor Mrs. McLaughlin did not once raise her head. Nellie, too, hid her pale face in her hands.

Dorothy was frightened, and when all were saying good-night she pressed a kiss on Nellie's cheek, and told her that the life-savers on Sunset Beach would surely be able to save all the sailors that came that way during the big storm.

Nellie and her mother occupied the same room. Of course the mother had been told that the long delayed boat had been sighted, and now, how anxiously she awaited more news of Nellie's father.

"We must not worry," she told Nellie, "for who knows but the storm may really help father's boat to get into port?"

So, while the waves lashed furiously upon Sunset Beach, all the people in the Minturn cottage were sleeping, or trying to sleep, for, indeed, it was not easy to rest when there was so much danger at their very door.

Life-savers

"Mother, mother!" called Nellie, "look down at the beach. The life-guards are burning the red signal lights! They have found a wreck!"

It was almost morning, but the black storm clouds held the daylight back. Mrs. McLaughlin and her little daughter strained their eyes to see, if possible, what might be going on down at the beach. While there was no noise to give the alarm, it seemed, almost everybody in that house felt the presence of the wreck, for in a very few minutes, Bert was at his window, Dorothy and Nan were looking out of theirs, while the older members of the household were dressing hastily, to see if they might be of any help in case of accident at the beach.

"Can I go with you, Uncle?" called Bert, who had heard his uncle getting ready to run down to the water's edge.

"Yes, come along," answered Mr. Minturn, and as day began to peep through the heavy clouds, the two hurried down to the spot where the life-guards were burning their red light to tell the sailors their signal had been seen.

"There's the vessel!" exclaimed Bert, as a rocket flew up from the water.

"Yes, that's the distress signal," replied the uncle. "It is lucky that daylight is almost here."

Numbers of other cottagers were hurrying to the scene now, Mr. Bingham and Hal being among the first to reach the spot.

"It's a schooner," said Mr. Bingham to Mr. Minturn, "and she has a very heavy cargo."

The sea was so wild it was impossible to send out the life-savers' boats, so the guards were making ready the breeches buoy.

"They are going to shoot the line out now," explained Hal to Bert, as the two-wheel car with the mortar or cannon was dragged down to the ocean's edge.

Instantly there shot out to sea a ball of thin cord. To this cord was fastened a heavy rope or cable.

"They've got it on the schooner." exclaimed a man, for the thin cord was now pulling the cable line out, over the water.

"What's that board for?" asked Bert, as he saw a board following the cable.

"That's the directions," said Hal.

"They are printed in a number of languages, and they tell the crew to carry the end of the cable high up the mast and fasten it strongly there."

"Oh, I see," said Bert, "the line will stretch then, and the breeches buoy will go out on a pulley."

"That's it," replied Hal. "See, there goes the buoy," and then the queer-looking life-preserver made of cork, and shaped like breeches, swung out over the waves.

It was clear day now, and much of the wicked storm had passed. Its effect upon the sea was, however, more furious every hour, for while the storm had left the land, it was raging somewhere else, and the sensitive sea felt every throb of the excited elements.

With the daylight came girls and women to the beach.

Mrs. Bobbsey, Mrs. Minturn, Nellie and her mother, besides Dorothy and Nan, were all there; Flossie and Freddie being obliged to stay home with Dinah and Susan.

Of course the girls asked all sorts of questions and Bert and Hal tried to answer them as best they could.

It seemed a long time before any movement of the cable showed that the buoy was returning.

"Here she comes! Here she comes!" called the crowd presently, as the black speck far out, and the strain on the cord, showed the buoy was coming back.

Up and down in the waves it bobbed, sometimes seeming to go all the way under. Nearer and nearer it came, until now a man's head could be seen.

"There's a man in it!" exclaimed the boys, all excitement, while the life-guards pulled the cord steadily, dragging in their human freight.

The girls and women were too frightened to talk, and Nellie clung close to her mother.

A big roller dashing in finished the work for the life-guards, and a man in the cork belt bounded upon shore.

He was quite breathless when the guards reached him, but insisted on walking up instead of being carried. Soon he recovered himself and the rubber protector was pulled off his face.

Everybody. gathered around, and Nellie with a strange face, and a stranger hope, broke through the crowd to see the rescued man.

"Oh—it is—*my*—*father!*" she screamed, falling right into the arms of the drenched man.

"Be careful," called Mr. Minturn, fearing the child might be mistaken, or Mrs. McLaughlin might receive too severe a shock from the surprise.

But the half-drowned man rubbed his eyes as if he could not believe them, then the next minute he pressed his little daughter to his heart, unable to speak a word.

What a wonderful scene it was!

The child almost unconscious in her father's arms, he almost dead from exhaustion, and the wife and mother too overcome to trust herself to believe it could be true.

Even the guards, who were busy again at the ropes, having left the man to willing hands on the beach, could not hide their surprise over the fact that it was mother, father, and daughter there united under such strange conditions.

"My darling, my darling!" exclaimed the sailor to Nellie, as he raised himself and then he saw his wife.

Mrs. Bobbsey had been holding Mrs. McLaughlin back, but now the sailor was quite recovered, so they allowed her to speak to him.

Mr. Bingham and Hal had been watching it all, anxiously.

"Are you McLaughlin?" suddenly asked Mr. Bingham.

"I am," replied the sailor.

"And is George Bingham out there?" anxiously asked the brother.

"Safe and well," came the welcome answer. "Just waiting for his turn to come in."

"Oh!" screamed Dorothy, "Hal's uncle is saved too. I guess our prayers were heard last night."

"Here comes another man!" exclaimed the people, as this time a big man dashed on the sands.

"All right!" exclaimed the man, as he landed, for he had had a good safe swing in, and was in no way exhausted.

"Hello there!" called Mr. Bingham: "Well, if this isn't luck. George Bingham!"

Sure enough it was Hal's Uncle George, and Hal was hugging the big wet man, while the man was jolly, and laughing as if the whole thing were a good joke instead of the life-and-death matter it had been.

"I only came in to tell you," began George Bingham, "that we are all right, and the boat is lifting off the sand bar we stuck on. But I'm glad I came in to—the reception," he said, laughing. "So you've found friends, McLaughlin," he added, seeing the little family united. "Why, how do you do, Mrs. McLaughlin?" he went on, offering her his hand. "And little Nellie! Well, I declare, we did land on a friendly shore."

Just as Mr. Bingham said, the life-saving work turned out to be a social affair, for there was a great time greeting Nellie's father and Hal's uncle.

"Wasn't it perfectly splendid that Nellie and her mother were here!" declared Dorothy.

"And Hal and his father, too," put in Nan. "It is just like a story in a book."

"But we don't have to look for the pictures," chimed in Bert, who was greatly interested in the sailors, as well as in the work of the life-saving corps.

As Mr. Bingham told the guards it would not be necessary to haul any more men in, and as the sea was calm enough now to launch a life-boat, both Nellie's father and Hal's uncle insisted on going back to the vessel to the other men.

Nellie was dreadfully afraid to have her father go out on the ocean again, but he only laughed at her fears, and said he would soon be in to port, to go home with her, and never go on the big, wild ocean again.

Two boats were launched, a strong guard going in each, with Mr. McLaughlin in one and Mr. Bingham in the other, and now they pulled out steadily over the waves, back to the vessel that was freeing itself from the sand bar.

What a morning that was at Sunset Beach!

The happiness of two families seemed to spread all through the little colony, and while the men were thinking of the more serious work of helping the sailors with their vessel, the girls and women were planning a great welcome for the men who had been saved from the waves.

"I'm so glad we prayed," said little Flossie to Freddie, when she heard the good news.

"It was Uncle William prayed the loudest," insisted Freddie, believing, firmly, that to reach heaven a long and loud prayer is always best.

"But we all helped," declared his twin sister, while surely the angels had listened to even the sleepy whisper of the little ones, who had asked help for the poor sailors in their night of peril.

The Happy Reunion

A beautiful day had grown out of the dreadful storm.

The sun seemed stronger each time it made its way out from behind a cloud, just as little girls and boys grow strong in body by exercise, and strong in character by efforts to do right.

And everybody was so happy.

The *Neptune*—the vessel that had struck on the sand bar—was now safely anchored near shore, and the sailors came in and out in row-boats, back and forth to land, just as they wished.

Of course Captain Bingham, Hal's uncle, was at the Bingham cottage, and the first mate, Nellie's father, was at Minturn's.

But that evening there was a regular party on Minturn's veranda. Numbers of cottagers called to see the sailors, and all were invited to remain and hear about the strange voyage of the *Neptune*.

"There is not much to tell," began the captain. "Of course I knew we were going to have trouble getting that mahogany. Two vessels had been wrecked trying to get it, so when we got to the West Indies I decided to try canoes and not risk sails, where the wind always blew such a gale, it dragged any anchor that could be dropped. Well, it was a long, slow job to drag those heavy logs around that point, and just when we were making headway, along comes a storm that drove the schooner and canoes out of business."

Here Mate McLaughlin told about the big storm and how long it took the small crew to repair the damage done to the sails.

"Then we had to go back to work at the logs," went on the captain, "and then one of our crew took a fever. Well, then we were quarantined. Couldn't get things to eat without a lot of trouble, and couldn't go on with the carting until the authorities decided the fever was not serious. That was what delayed us so.

"Finally, we had every log loaded on the schooner and we started off. But I never could believe any material would be as heavy as that mahogany; why, we just had to creep along, and the least contrary wind left us motionless on the sea.

"We counted on getting home last week, when this last storm struck us and drove us out of our course. But we are not sorry for our delay now, since we have come back to our own."

"About the value?" asked Mr. Bobbsey, who was down from the city.

"The value," repeated the captain aside, so that the strangers might not hear. "Well, I'm a rich man now, and so is my mate, McLaughlin, for that wood was contracted for by the largest and richest piano firm in this country, and now it is all but delivered to them and the money in our hands."

"Then it was well worth all your sacrifice?" said Mr. Minturn.

"Yes, indeed. It would have taken us a lifetime to accumulate as much money as we have earned in this year. Of course, it was hard for the men who had families, McLaughlin especially; the others were all working sailors, but he was a landsman and my partner in the enterprise; but I will make it up to him, and the mahogany hunt will turn out the best paying piece of work he ever undertook."

"Oh, isn't it perfectly splendid!" declared Nan and Dorothy, hugging Nellie. "You will never again have to go back to that horrid store that made you so pale, and your mother will have a lovely time and nothing to worry about."

"I can hardly believe it all," replied their little friend. "But having father back is the very best of all."

"But all the same," sighed Dorothy, "I just know you will all be going home before we leave for the city, and I shall just die of loneliness."

"But we have to go to school," said Nan, "and we have only a few days more."

"Of course," continued Dorothy; "and our school will not open for two weeks yet."

"Maybe Aunt Emily will take you down to the city on her shopping tour," suggested Nan.

"Indeed I do not like shopping," answered the cousin. "Every time I go in a store that is crowded with stuff on the counters under people's elbows, I feel like knocking the things all over. I did a lot of damage that way once. It was holiday time, and a counter that stuck out in the middle of the store was full of little statues. My sleeve touched one, and the whole lot fell down as if a cannon had struck them. I broke ten and injured more than I wanted to count."

"And Aunt Emily had to pay for them?" said Nan.

"No, she didn't, either," corrected Dorothy. "The manager came up and said the things should not be put out in people's way. He made the clerks remove all the truck from the aisles and I guess everybody was glad the army fell down. I never can forget those pink-and-white soldiers," and Dorothy straightened herself up in comical "soldier's arms" fashion, imitating the unfortunate statues.

"I hope you can come to Lakeport for Thanksgiving," said Nan. "We have done so much visiting this summer, out to Aunt Sarah's and down here, mamma feels we ought to have a grand reunion at our house next. If we do, I am going to try to have some of the country girls down and give them all a jolly good time."

"Oh, I'll come if you make it jolly," answered Dorothy. "If there is one thing in this world worth while, it is fun," and she tossed her yellow head about like a buttercup, that has no other way of laughing.

That had been an eventful day at Ocean Cliff, and the happy ending of it, with a boat and its crew saved, was, as some of the children said, just like a story in a book, only the pictures were all alive!

The largest hotel at Sunset Beach was thrown open to the sailors that night, and here Captain Bingham and Mate McLaughlin, together with the rest of the crew, took up comfortable lodgings.

It was very late, long after the little party had scattered from Minturn's piazza, that the sailors finished dancing their hornpipe for the big company assembled to greet them in the hotel.

Never had they danced to such fine music before, for the hotel orchestra played the familiar tune and the sailors danced it nimbly, hitching up first one side then the other—crossing first one leg then the other, and wheeling around in that jolly fashion.

How rugged and handsome the men looked! The rough ocean winds had tanned them like bronze, and their muscles were as firm and strong almost as the cables that swing out with the buoys. The wonderful fresh air that these men lived in, night and day, had brightened their eyes too, so that even the plainest face, and the most awkward man among them, was as nimble as an athlete, from his perfect exercise.

"And last night what an awful experience they had!" remarked one of the spectators. "It is no wonder that they are all so happy to-night."

"Besides," added someone else, "they are all going to receive extra good pay, for the captain and mate will be very rich when the cargo is landed."

So the sailors danced until they were tired, and then after a splendid meal they went to sleep, in as comfortable beds as might be found in any hotel on Sunset Beach.

Good-by

"I don't know how to say good-by to you," Nellie told Dorothy and Nan next morning. "To think how kind you have been to me, and how splendidly it has all turned out! Now father is home again, I can hardly believe it! Mother told me last night she was going to put back what money she had to use out of my prize, the fifty dollars you know, and I am to make it a gift to the Fresh Air Fund."

"Oh, that will be splendid!" declared Nan. "Perhaps they will buy another tent with it, for they need more room out at Meadow Brook."

"You are quite rich now, aren't you?" remarked Dorothy. "I suppose your father will buy a big house, and maybe next time we meet you, you will put on airs and walk like this?" and Dorothy went up and down the room like the pictures of Cinderella's proud sisters.

"No danger," replied Nellie, whose possible tears at parting had been quickly chased away by the merry Dorothy. "But I hope we will have a nice home, for mother deserves it, besides I am just proud enough to want to entertain a few young ladies, among them Miss Nan Bobbsey and Miss Dorothy Minturn."

"And we will be on hand, thank you," replied the joking Dorothy. "Be sure to have ice cream and chocolates—I want some good fresh chocolates. Those we get down here always seem soft and salty, like the spray."

"Come, Nellie," called Mrs. McLaughlin, "I am ready. Where is your hat?"

"Oh, yes, mother, I'm coming!" replied Nellie.

Bert had the donkey cart hitched and there was now no time to spare. Nellie kissed Freddie and Flossie affectionately, and promised to bring the little boy all through a big city, real fire-engine house when he came to see her.

"And can I ring the bell and make the horses jump?" he asked.

"We might be able to manage that, too," Nellie told him. "My uncle is a fireman and he can take us through his engine house."

Nan went to the station with her friends, and when the last good-bys were said and the train steamed out, the twins turned back again to the Minturn Cottage.

"Our turn next," remarked Bert, as he pulled the donkeys into the drive.

"Yes, it seems it is nothing but going and coming all the time. I wonder if all the other girls will be home at Lakeport in time for the first day of school?" said Nan.

"Most of them, I guess," answered Bert. "Well, we have had a good vacation, and I am willing to go to work again."

"So am I!" declared Nan. "Vacation was just long enough, I think."

Mr. Bobbsey was down from the city, of course, to take the family home, and now all hands, even Freddie and Flossie, were busy packing up. There were the shells to be looked after, the fish nets, besides Downy, the duck, and Snoop, the cat.

"And just to add one more animal to your menagerie," said Uncle William, "I have brought you a little goldfinch. It will sing beautifully for you, and be easy to carry in its little wooden cage. Then, I have ordered, sent directly to your house, a large cage for him to live in, so he will have plenty of freedom, and perhaps Christmas you may get some more birds to put in the big house, to keep Dick company."

Of course Freddie was delighted with the gift, for it was really a beautiful little bird, with golden wings, and a much prettier pet than a duck or a cat, although he still loved his old friends.

The day passed very quickly with all that was crowded into it: the last ocean bath taking up the best part of two hours, while a sail in Hal's canoe did away with almost as much, more time. Dorothy gave Nan a beautiful little gold locket with her picture in it, and Flossie received the dearest little real shell pocketbook ever seen. Hal Bingham gave Bert a magnifying glass, to use at school in chemistry or physics, so that every one of the Bobbseys received a suitable souvenir of Sunset Beach.

"You-uns must be to bed early and not go sleep in de train," insisted Dinah, when Freddie and Flossie pleaded for a little more time on the veranda that evening. "Come along now; Dinah hab lots to do too," and with her little charges the good-natured colored girl hobbled off, promising to tell Freddie how Nellie's father and Hal's uncle were to get into port again when they set out to sea, instead of trying to get the big boat into land at Sunset Beach.

And so our little friends had spent all their vacation.

The last night at the seashore was passed, and the early morning found them once more traveling away—this time for dear old home, sweet home.

"If we only didn't have to leave our friends," complained Nan, brushing back a tear, as the very last glint of Cousin Dorothy's yellow head passed by the train window.

"I hope we will meet them all soon again," said Nan's mother. "It is not long until Thanksgiving. Then, perhaps, we can give a real harvest party out at Lakeport and try to repay our friends for some of their hospitality to us."

"Well, I like Hal Bingham first-rate," declared Bert, thinking of the friend from whom he had just parted.

"There goes the last of the ocean. Look!" called Flossie, as the train made a turn, and whistled a good-by to the Bobbsey Twins at the Seashore.

Made in the USA
Coppell, TX
05 September 2021

61858704R10059